you are here

Jennifer E. Smith

Simon & Schuster Books for Young Readers
New York   London   Toronto   Sydney

Also by Jennifer E. Smith

The Comeback Season

SIMON & SCHUSTER BOOKS FOR YOUNG READERS
An imprint of Simon & Schuster Children's Publishing Division
1230 Avenue of the Americas, New York, New York 10020

Book design by Krista Vossen
The text for this book is set in Fournier.
Manufactured in the United States of America
2 4 6 8 10 9 7 5 3 1
Library of Congress Cataloging-in-Publication Data
Smith, Jennifer E.
You are here / Jennifer E. Smith.—1st ed.
p. cm.
Summary: Sixteen-year-old Emma Healy has never felt that she fit in with the rest of her family, so when she discovers that she had a twin brother who died shortly after they were born, she takes off on an impulsive road trip to try to discover who she really is.
ISBN: 978-1-4169-6799-6
[1. Automobile travel—Fiction. 2. Identity—Fiction.
3. Individuality—Fiction. 4. Death—Fiction. 5. Twins—Fiction.
6. Family—Fiction. 7. Dogs—Fiction.] I. Title.
PZ7.S65141Yo 2009
[Fic]—dc22
2008027071

FIRST
EDITION

To my family

chapter one

Still somewhat to her surprise, Emma Healy had started off the morning by stealing her older brother's car.

This was not an impulsive decision. It wasn't something she'd come up with the night before while lying on the couch in his New York City apartment, watching the numbers on the microwave clock shift and re-form as the light outside the window paled to gray. Though the last thing she'd ever stolen was a pack of bubble gum in the third grade, and though most of her plans had a habit of fizzling out along the way, Emma had already known with a kind of solemn certainty that as soon as the sun was fully up, she would slip on her shoes, tiptoe out the door, and drive off in Patrick's car.

What she *hadn't* known was that it would break down so quickly, not fifty miles out of the city, at a New Jersey rest stop, where she now sat perched on a picnic table, regarding the smoke seeping from the hood of the blue convertible, trying to figure out her next move.

She probably should have known better. The Mustang wasn't exactly the most obvious choice for a getaway car. Patrick had bought it when he was her age, nearly fifteen years ago, which made it not quite old enough to be vintage, though not new enough to run properly. It was like a moving junkyard, a clanging chorus of coughs and belches, and it had a baffling tendency to stall, though it wasn't even stick shift. Patrick was practically a full-fledged mechanic at this point for the number of times he'd paged through the manuals, trying to fix the ornery vehicle himself.

But even so, almost from the moment he'd arrived home in it just a few days ago, sputtering up to the house nearly an hour late for the Fourth of July party, a plan had begun to take shape in the farthest corners of Emma's mind, like an itch she couldn't quite scratch.

"It sounds like your car ate a lawn mower," she'd said, traipsing down the front path to greet him.

"I keep telling her to stop chasing smaller machines, but she never listens," he said, thumping the hood with a grin. Like all three of her older siblings, Patrick was in his thirties and spectacularly odd in his own way. He had more diplomas and less common sense than anyone she'd ever known. He was working toward a second PhD in some obscure field that combined philosophy and math, but when she'd last visited him in New York, he'd barely been able to load the dishwasher or manage a grocery list. Emma often wondered whether the price of such intelligence was losing all normal logic. It seemed to be the case in her family, at least, and she'd long ago given up trying to understand their peculiar tendencies. That was a science in and of itself.

"Sorry I'm late," he'd said, looking off toward the back-yard, where the annual cookout was underway, the smell of hot dogs heavy in the air and the smoke from the barbecue twisting skyward.

"Oh, yeah, I'm sure you are," Emma said, and Patrick laughed.

"It's nice having an unreliable car," he said, giving the tire a little kick. "Gives you an excuse to be unreliable yourself."

The party was, as always, a sorry affair. Nobody was throwing water balloons or waving sparklers or even wearing red, white, and blue. Nobody was fishing through the cooler for another can of beer, and nobody had spilled any ketchup, aside from the eighty-eight-year-old former dean of the college, who had fallen asleep holding his hamburger.

Instead, a few members of the English department were arguing with a new history professor over the relevance of texts from the time of the Revolutionary War, two men in shirtsleeves were debating the exact words of a long-dead poet, and Emma's parents were holding forth on their recent trip to Patagonia, where Mom had done fieldwork on historical burial sites and Dad had put the finishing touches on his latest collection of poetry.

Down the road the last stragglers from the parade were making their way past the rows of houses that lined the main street into town, where small clapboard homes like the Healys' began to give way to fraternity row, each mansion bigger than the next, with columns and gabled roofs displaying fading Greek letters like badges of affluence. Beyond them the college sat high on the hill, and Emma could see the sun glancing off the bell tower of the chapel.

"I'm probably too old for this thing anyway," Patrick said, turning back to the car.

"You should get a new one then," Emma suggested. "You could leave this one up here for me." She knew it was a long shot, but she was sixteen—almost seventeen—and stranded in upstate New York for the summer, the first inklings of a plan already springing to life as she regarded the balding tires of the convertible. If old was what it took to convince him to give up his car, then she had no intention of contradicting him.

"For you?" he said, trying not to smile. He rapped his knuckles on the rearview mirror. "This thing would be toast in under a week."

"No way," Emma said, straightening her shoulders. "I'm a really good driver. You're just never around to see."

She'd grown used to her family underestimating her. It was like this with everything. Emma had never even been allowed so much as a hamster, because her parents always insisted she was too irresponsible to care for a pet. Instead she'd had to make do with a series of seemingly suicidal goldfish, whose rapid succession of deaths did little to help her case in lobbying for a puppy.

"Don't think so," Patrick said, glancing down at the car. "Besides, I can't afford another one. I can barely even afford this one. I mean, do you have any idea how much it costs to keep a car in the city? If you add the price of gas to the cost of parking—obviously adjusting for the days when I mange to actually find a spot on the street—plus the insurance, not to mention all those stupid tickets . . ."

"Patrick."

He paused, his mouth still half open. "Yeah?"

"Can we not calculate it just now?"

He nodded, his face slipping into the kind of distant smile her whole family used when regarding Emma, like she was a foreign object that had somehow fallen in their midst.

"Must be tough being the baby, huh?" he said eventually, and Emma shrugged.

"It's a lot tougher being the only normal one."

Later, once Mom and Dad finally dragged Patrick off to the backyard to regale their colleagues with stories of his program at Columbia, Emma wandered off on her own. She was fairly certain nobody would notice her absence. It was surprisingly easy to get lost in her family, and not just today; their home was constantly filled with other professors and neighbors, visiting writers, and students with questions about their essays. There was always a fire going or a kettle of tea on the stove or a book available for borrowing. Theirs was a house where independence was encouraged, where coming in past curfew didn't result in any punishment other than the possibility of getting roped into a late-night discussion about the origin of a certain plant.

Emma had learned early on how to make herself scarce. It wasn't terribly difficult; her parents were often lost in the library for days at a time, and all three of her older siblings had moved out when she was little. She'd never known them in the way other kids know their brothers and sisters; there was no fighting for seats in the car or playing tag in the backyard until it was too dark to see. Her oldest brother, Nate, had left for college soon after she was born, and the others followed shortly afterward.

Emma saw them now only on occasional visits or major holidays, and she felt as undone in their company as she sometimes did with her parents. Nate, the ecologist, was always lecturing her on a range of impressive but boring subjects, and Annie—her only sister, who should have been the one she called for advice about boys, but who instead made her so worried about saying something stupid that Emma could barely talk around her—was a government engineer in Washington. And then, of course, there was Patrick, who collected degrees like baseball cards and had an exasperating habit of calculating everything out loud.

Her mom and dad had spent much of their academic careers moving from one university to the next, and their children ended up settling in the various places they'd once lived, landing in North Carolina, Washington DC, and New York City like passengers stepping off a northbound train. Emma was grateful her parents had managed to get tenure here—at this small liberal arts school just a stone's throw away from absolutely nothing at all—or else it was just as likely they'd have continued moving north until they hit a tundra somewhere in Newfoundland.

But even when she was very young, Emma could recognize the differences between herself and the rest of her family. They'd lived an entire life without her, countless birthdays and family squabbles and summer vacations— but it wasn't just that. When she first started school, instead of getting notes with smiley faces in her lunch box, Emma used to find slips of paper with quotes from famous philosophers. Instead of a new sweater for Christmas, she'd get a heavy volume of poetry or a rock-polishing kit. At the dinner table her parents talked about Proust or pi rather than anything normal, like baseball games or plans for the weekend. They couldn't comment on the weather without remarking on the low air pressure or the worsening state of the ozone layer, and when Emma once broke her arm on the swing set, her dad had recited the poetry of W. H. Auden on the way to the hospital in an attempt to calm her down.

All her life Emma had felt alone in her family. She'd perfected a look of detached but polite interest, had developed a basic vocabulary to survive dinners when her siblings were home, and had resigned herself to her role as the youngest and least bright of a slightly odd but inarguably brilliant family. And though this was all a bit exhausting, it had never occurred to her to question it. Until last week.

Just six days earlier Dad had asked her to go up to the attic to find his early editions of W. B. Yeats for an article he was working on. Even after eight years in this house it seemed that very few of her parents' books had actually made it to the shelves where they belonged. There were books in the attic, the basement, the garage; books stacked to create tables and footstools and doorstops all over the house. Each time a quote was needed, a vaguely remembered reference or a line from a novel, Emma was sent off in search of its source, a task not unlike a scavenger hunt.

And so, at her dad's request, she'd climbed the ladder to the attic, then set about rummaging through the assortment of cardboard boxes, crouching on the wooden planks of the crawl space and trying not to sneeze. There were bags full of old stuffed animals and shoes, a faded globe and a tiny rocking horse. The afternoon light filtered in through the lone window, and though she could see the boxes of books tucked way in the back, Emma soon got sidetracked picking through the ones with photo albums and scrapbooks.

She sat cross-legged on the floor of the attic, paging through pictures of her siblings when they lived in North Carolina, the three of them nearly unrecognizable as kids, running through sprinklers in saggy bathing suits, playing in the backyard of the house where Emma had once lived as a baby. After a while, Dad seemed to give up on her—his footsteps receding back down the stairs—and so she reached in and fished around for something more, rare glimpses of a past that didn't include her.

There was another box within the bigger one, a small shoebox that opened with a little cough of dust. Inside was a stack of papers, some of them wrinkled, others pressed flat, and Emma held them up to the light one at a time: old school reports and handmade birthday cards, a love letter Dad had written to Mom before they were married, and various announcements of honors and awards. Toward the bottom she discovered Nate's birth certificate, and she traced a finger over the letters and smiled, already reaching for the next one. She glanced at Annie's and then Patrick's, too, and when she got to her own, she studied it carefully, fingering the edges of the rough paper, the announcement of Emma Quinn Healy's arrival into the world. It wasn't until she twisted to pick up the pile she'd made on the floor beside her that she noticed there was still one left in the box.

The name on the paper said Thomas Quinn Healy. And his birth date, printed in neat black letters along the bottom, was exactly the same as hers.

Emma's thoughts assembled themselves slowly in her head, and she had, for the briefest of moments, a fleeting sense of understanding. *Finally*, she thought, looking at the fifth birth certificate in her hands. There was finally an answer to all those years of loneliness, a reason for the vague feeling she'd always had that something was missing.

But before she had a chance to wonder all the things she would have wondered—a mysterious brother, a long lost twin, all the deep, dark secrets of childhood revealed—she found the other piece of paper, the very last one in the box: a death certificate dated just two days later.

chapter two

As he looped beneath the highway and swung onto the road leading to the New Jersey Turnpike, Peter Finnegan was reassured by the sound of the maps flapping in the backseat, twisting in the wind as if trying to take flight. Some were rolled and fastened with rubber bands; others were folded neatly and pinned down by small stacks of books. Peter hadn't just brought directions for the tristate area, but also guides to Moscow and London and Sydney, not because he planned to visit there—not on *this* trip, anyway—but because there was a certain comfort in them. They were creased and fraying and worn, but it was still easy to lose himself in the lines and keys and markings, the gentle scribblings of rivers and the sharper points of the mountains. He never felt so sure of his place in the world as when he pinpointed it on an atlas.

Back home in upstate New York, Peter's bedroom was much the same. It looked a lot like the last outpost to some unexplored region of the world, or else the situation room of a government agency, strewn with maps and notes and thumbtacks as if something—either a great war or a great discovery—were imminent. Some of the maps were fairly basic, with states the color of bubble gum peering up at him from opened books on the floor beside his bed, the kind of sunshiny atlases where the lakes and rivers are so blue you nearly expect a fish to poke his head out and wave a fin in greeting. Most of these were left over from Peter's younger days, when he'd made a game out of memorizing the state capitals, inventing characters out of the names: Ms. Helena Montana, the old woman who sat rocking herself to sleep on a porch overlooking the mountains, or Mr. Montgomery Alabama, the slow-talking Southern gentleman who could always be counted on to wear his finest suit.

But there were other maps too. Road maps, with their unruly lines, and topographical ones with rings upon rings circling the sunken paper mountains like the inside of an ancient tree. Some showed the climate, and others marked off national treasures or parks. A few focused in on specific towns, while others panned out to include the entire country, welcoming the pale oceans that crept into the frame on either side. There were a few yellowing military maps from various time periods, and even one dating back to the Civil War, unearthed last summer at the local farmers' market.

The shelves that lined the rest of the room featured a combination of required reading for school—*The Catcher in the Rye, The Great Gatsby, The Grapes of Wrath*—and an astonishing assortment of books about cartography, geography, and of course the Civil War, another peculiar fascination of Peter's. It was sometimes hard to know which had

11

come first, the maps or the soldiers, but somewhere along the way they'd come to coexist, and now along the edges of the shelves there were lines of little metal soldiers dressed in blue and gray, who had to be nudged aside each time you needed a book, running the risk of a domino effect, the possibility of an entire fallen unit.

Peter was not unaware of how all this looked. Not only could it pass for the room of the nerdiest kid in school—an observation not wholly inaccurate—but it might very well be mistaken for the home of some delusional nutcase who appeared to be making preparations for a march back through time, as if hoping to follow the carefully outlined maps straight back into the Battle of Antietam.

Peter, however, had no such plans.

Though this is not to say he didn't have other ones. In fact Peter Finnegan had more plans than anyone he knew. And not the normal kind, the *see you after school* or *what are you doing Saturday night?* or *meet me in the cafeteria* kind.

Instead Peter planned to go to Australia and Africa and Alaska and Antarctica, and that was just the *A*s. The list grew from there, ballooning to include Bali and Bangladesh, China and California and Chicago. He had marked carefully on the map the place where you might catch a ferry from Ireland to Scotland, had researched mountain climbing in Switzerland and cage diving with sharks off the coast of South Africa. He'd included places like Boston, too, Maine and Canada and even Boise, where he would sample potatoes dipped in butter or ketchup, potatoes fried, peeled, boiled, mashed, and baked. It didn't matter that he wasn't a fan of the potatoes Dad cooked back in upstate New York. They'd be different in Boise. That's what happened when you clawed away the drab details of your real life and shed them for something different, something more exciting and altogether more real. *That's* when life really started. In some faraway place, exotic or rustic, foreign or familiar— but somewhere, elsewhere, anywhere but here.

"What's the point?" Dad would say whenever Peter slid a travel magazine across the dinner table, or showed him some advertisement for a sale on airline tickets or a kids-stay-free deal at a roadside motel. "You want to pay for a crappy room with a broken mattress and a moldy shower-head, when you can stay in the comfort of your own home for free?"

He'd sweep an arm across the kitchen to demonstrate those very comforts, highlighting the rusty faucet and partially unhinged cabinets with all the enthusiasm of a game-show host. The whole house—which they'd moved into just after Peter was born and his mother died, events separated only by minutes, a double feature of joy and tragedy that had forever confused that day—was decorated in various shades of green, which had faded over the years to give the place an algae-like feeling, gauzy and faded, like they were living in a long-forgotten shipwreck under the sea.

Peter was hard-pressed to pick out the so-called comforts of the place, and thought a change of scenery—a sea-side cottage in Cape Cod, or a tourist trap near the Grand Canyon—might do them both a great deal of good. But Dad seemed just as content to flop down on the couch each night after work, still decked out in his police uniform, so that he looked like an extra in one of those TV shows, an officer thrown aside as the criminal makes his break. For him the comforts of home included a can of beer, a bowl of

13

peanuts, and a baseball game with the volume turned low enough that he might dip in and out of sleep.

And so, until today, the only place checked off Peter's list—which took up half a spiral notebook, including addendums and footnotes—was New York City, which he'd once visited with his class on the biannual school field trip. He'd been just nine, and had fallen asleep on the bus ride down—something that later seemed horribly unfair, like he'd been swindled by his heavy eyelids—and had missed the scenery, though he could have quite easily directed the bus driver from Route 12 to I-87 and straight on into the city without thinking twice.

But it was the outside world he'd most wanted to see, the river gorges and hillsides that marked a transition from one place to another. When he woke up, enormous buildings had sprouted on either side of the bus as if by magic, and he'd spent the day trailing after the rest of his class in an unblinking daze. On the way home he'd somehow fallen asleep again, lulled by the rocking motion of the bus, and Hank Green had put a straw up his nose, and Liza and Maggie Kessler—evil twins if there ever were—had drawn a handlebar mustache on his face with red marker that took three days to rub out completely.

His class had gone back three times since then, but that was Peter's only trip. The second time he'd had chicken pox, and he'd come down with a bad case of strep throat on the third. Last year he'd been excluded as a punishment for "smart-mouthing" his teacher, though he'd only been trying to correct her after she repeatedly mispronounced "fallback plan," describing the Union's second-day battle strategy at Gettysburg as a "fall-*black* plan." Afterward, when she'd sent him to the principal's office, Peter had refused to admit to the "heckling" he was accused of and therefore sat in mute silence until his dad arrived, his badge prominently displayed, looking vaguely pleased at the idea of his son's first foray into troublemaking. Peter had always suspected his father would have known better how to raise a kid who threw eggs at people's windshields or set off stink bombs in the school bathroom. As it was, the man had no clue how to deal with a too-skinny, bespectacled boy who somehow preferred maps and battlefields to baseball and video games.

They'd fashioned a sort of invisible line inside the house, which seemed to work for them most of the time. Dad rarely appeared at Peter's door or questioned where he'd been when he spent his summer afternoons wandering around town. And in return Peter was careful to tiptoe around the crumpled figure of his father in the evenings, occasionally throwing away an empty beer can or refilling the bowl of peanuts if he was feeling generous.

So just the other day when there was a knock on Peter's door, he looked up from his maps in surprise. He'd been planning not a trek through the Himalayas or a walkabout in the Australian outback but just a short jaunt north to Canada, to Montreal or Quebec, where he might cross the border as confidently and casually as if he were a purveyor of maple syrup, or perhaps a hockey aficionado, who had been doing it his whole life.

"I thought you were gonna take out the garbage," Dad said, staring at the array of flattened maps that tiled the floor. "What, did you get lost or something?"

He laughed as if the joke had only just occurred to him, though he tended to use it at least once or twice a week, and it had long stopped being even remotely funny to Peter, who simply chose to ignore him. After a moment Dad's mouth snapped back into a straight line, and he put on his aviator glasses, despite the dimness of the room. "So, planning your big escape?"

Peter sat back on his heels. "I'm not trying to escape," he said, knowing this wasn't entirely true. "Though it might be nice to go *somewhere*."

"You know, not everyone can afford to just pick up and go somewhere whenever they want," Dad said, with a somewhat contemptuous look at the maps spread out like blueprints at his feet. "Not everyone has the means to just go traipsing around the globe."

Peter braced himself for yet another lecture about the many vices of those with money, the students who clogged the town each fall, the professors who taught them, the very notion of stipends and trust funds and endowments. Dad believed in a hard day's work and building character and home cooking (in theory, at least). He believed in responsibility and cleaning up your own mess and having a strong work ethic. He believed in being homegrown and salt of the earth. He hated high horses.

But for once the speech went no further. Instead he turned to Peter, gazed across that wide gulf between them, a body of water both dangerous and deep, home to man-eating fish and life-threatening creatures that made the idea of ever crossing seem far-fetched at best.

"You want to be careful about wandering," he said, as if giving a presentation to a group of second graders about to embark on a nature walk. "It's a good way to get yourself lost."

chapter three

It was nearly lunchtime when the car had begun to falter, a sound like someone dragging a metal trash can to the end of the driveway. There was a buckling feeling, like the whole vehicle was struggling to stay in motion, and Emma lifted her foot and listened to the engine heave, then counted to twenty with her eyes fixed on the dashboard. By the time she reached eighteen, the red emergency light had blinked on, and she felt her heart quicken as she merged into the slow lane and coasted toward the rest area, trying not to think of what Patrick might do to her if she ruined his car for good.

But just as soon as it had come on, the light went off again, and the car chugged up the incline with admirable determination. Emma maneuvered into a parking spot beside a camper van and breathed a sigh of relief as she switched off the ignition.

The trip, it seemed, wasn't over just yet.

The rest stop consisted of five different fast-food places and a gift shop, with outdoor picnic tables and a set of bathrooms she could smell from the parking lot. Emma decided to let the car recuperate while she had lunch, and made her way up to the crowded building, an A-frame structure that looked as if the architects had hoped people might forget they were not at a ski lodge in Vermont but rather at a rest stop on the Jersey Turnpike.

She waited in line at a burger stand amid the noisy thrum of people, bleary-eyed mothers and kids covered in ketchup and weary truck drivers who stretched their legs and yawned and seemed to be enjoying the diversion from the road. Emma ordered a burger and fries and then carried her tray past the orange plastic tables and arcade games to the glass door that led outside. There were six picnic tables on the side of the building farthest from the highway, and most were already occupied by families wearing shirts with the names of the various states they'd traveled through. Emma took a seat at the last open table, dabbing uselessly at a puddle of spilled soda with her napkin before unwrapping her burger.

This whole thing had started just yesterday morning, while Patrick was packing up his car to return to the city after spending a couple of days at home. Emma had been planning to go with him all along, ever since he'd shown up in the Mustang and the idea to steal it had first occurred to her, but she'd thought it better to spring it on everyone at the last minute. So when she showed up to say good-bye with a backpack slung over one shoulder, everyone stared at her. Emma smiled back at them brightly, then tossed her bag into the trunk.

"And where might you be going?" Patrick asked, raising one eyebrow.

"I thought I'd come stay with you for the weekend."

He laughed, but not like it was funny. "I've got my summer research stuff to finish up this weekend," he said. "And I'm teaching two classes on Monday that I still need to prepare for."

"I'll stay out of your way," she said. "I promise. It's just that there's *nothing* to do around here, and I thought it might be fun."

Dad looked equally unsure. "What about work?"

Emma's job as a camp counselor had fallen through when not enough kids showed up on the first day, so he'd hired her as a research assistant to pass the time over the summer. This basically meant running back and forth between home and the library to fetch and return books. She was pretty sure he could survive without her.

"You'll be busy finishing up your revisions anyhow," Mom reminded him. "And I've got my article to write. Maybe it's not such a bad idea. The house will be quieter this way."

Emma thought to point out that as noisy teenagers go, she fell pretty low on the scale, but decided against it. New York was only the first step in her plan, and if she were to mess things up now, before even really having a chance to begin, she'd be stuck at home for the rest of the summer with nothing to do but wonder about things from afar.

Ever since she found the birth certificate, she hadn't been able to shake the feeling that she should go down to North Carolina. Her grandfather was buried in a cemetery not far from Nate's house—in the same town where she'd been born—and though she'd never been there before, there was no reason not to think that Thomas Quinn Healy was buried there too.

She wasn't sure what she hoped to find. It was just a feeling she had, that she should make the trip. She had two parents and three siblings, none of whom understood her at all. Emma felt she owed it to the one brother who might have known her better to pay him a visit. It was as simple as that.

The night before, she'd trailed around the backyard after Mom, helping to clean up after the party and trying to figure out how to ask the question on her mind without really asking anything at all. Mom had always had a tendency to be vague and tight-lipped about the past; she'd never been the type to carry baby pictures in her wallet or tell childhood anecdotes at the dinner table. Emma had always assumed this was because she—like the rest of them—was too focused on her work to see anything outside of it. But now she realized that in the hiding of whatever had happened back then—the disappearance of her twin brother from the family story—other things must have gotten lost as well.

"Do you ever miss North Carolina?" she'd begun, finally, and Mom had stiffened. She was holding a soda can between two fingers, and it took her a moment to let go, dropping it into a garbage bag with a loud clink.

"I guess so," she said. "But no more than any of the other places we've lived. Plus, your brother's still down there, so we get to visit—"

"My brother?"

"Nate," Mom said, giving her a funny look. "What's up with you?"

Emma shrugged, torn between the desire to ask more and the fear that it might ruin her plans. She'd already made up her mind about driving to North Carolina, and while there was no doubt that it was completely irrational—it was foolish and illogical and probably more than a little bit stupid—she was just restless enough not to care. She wanted to go somewhere unknown and unfamiliar, somewhere farther than the college, beyond the hill and outside of this town. Quite simply, she wanted to *go*.

The plan was simple. She'd borrow Patrick's car in New York (this sounded far more harmless than stealing it) and then stop in DC, where she could stay with Annie, finally working her way down to North Carolina, where Nate and his fiancée lived in the same house her parents once had. If everything worked out, she could be there in a week, just in time for her seventeenth birthday. And after so many years of unsatisfying birthdays—of wishing for goody bags and pin-the-tail-on-the-donkey and yellow cake with chocolate frosting, but instead getting encyclopedias and magnifying glasses and leather-bound poetry collections—where better to spend it than with the one person who'd once shared the day with her?

It didn't, in the end, take as much convincing as she'd expected before Patrick finally caved, and they'd only been on the road for half an hour before she'd gotten him to agree to spend the rest of the afternoon with her too. They left the top down on the convertible, though the rush of air made it too loud to talk, and they drove on with chapped lips and wind-burned faces, their bare elbows dangling over the doors as the landscape reeled past. They passed low-slung barns and crumbling silos, the little car groaning each time it crested a hill, only to fall again with a resigned whirring noise.

It took more than an hour to emerge from the depths of the forgotten half of the state of New York and onto the main expressway, where they left behind the rambling fields and wooden fences for the highways with their sharp medians and yellow lines of paint.

"So what should we do this afternoon?" Patrick asked, once the wind had died down enough for them to talk. "Central Park? Brooklyn Bridge? How about the Met? There's a great exhibit on now. Contemporary art."

Emma rolled her eyes. "I hate museums."

"Oh, come on," he said. "Nobody *hates* museums."

"Well, nobody actually *likes* them, either," she said. "It's the kind of thing people like to say they've done, but don't really like doing."

Patrick laughed. "That's absurd."

"So is contemporary art," said Emma, unmoved.

"Okay, so what's *your* brilliant plan for the day?"

Emma looked off to where the quilted landscape around the road had begun to gather itself in gray-brown clusters of shopping malls and car dealerships, dizzying billboards and the occasional office complex. The sun was bright against the distant city, which rose black and uneven beyond a labyrinth of bridges. She held her breath against the smell of it, the faint stench of garbage and exhaust that drifted over from New Jersey, the sudden closeness of the buildings that stifled the air around them.

This was the city where she'd lived when she was little, where she'd gone to kindergarten in a plaid skirt and played soccer on a field near the highway, where she'd learned to ride a bike on the uneven sidewalk outside their West Village apartment. By the time her parents made it up to Manhattan to take teaching positions at NYU and Columbia, all three of Emma's brothers and sisters were gone, off to college or else already impressing a new audience of adoring bosses and coworkers. But this was where Emma had lived from the time she was five until she was eight, and so now she realized she had no interest in seeing Times Square. She didn't want to visit the Statue of Liberty or Ellis Island or any of the other landmarks that told stories of the city's past. And she certainly didn't want to go to the Met.

For once, it was her own past that she was concerned about, and it suddenly seemed important to connect the dots on her way to North Carolina, to discover not just the beginning, but the other chapters as well, the checkered timeline of a history that was dangerously close to being forgotten.

"Can we go see the old apartment?"

Patrick raised his eyebrows. "Feeling nostalgic?"

"A little," she admitted, turning back to the skyline unfurling before the little car.

Later, after they'd parked and dropped their bags at Patrick's and taken the long subway ride down the west side of Manhattan, the two of them stood before a building on the corner of Greenwich and Bank streets. Emma ran her eyes up the burnt-colored bricks to the fourth window on the right, and then below that to the gum-stained steps, where she used to sit twisting a jump rope around the wrought-iron railings.

"I'm pretty sure it was this one, right?" Patrick was saying, backpedaling to get a better look. "It's been forever, huh?"

Emma moved her chin just slightly. Beside a pile of garbage bags a few pigeons picked at someone's leftover pizza, and Patrick took a seat on the top stair, stubbing the toe of his shoe against a crumpled cigarette on the ground.

"I guess I wasn't around much when we lived here."

"I know," Emma said, and the way she said it—so quietly, as much an accusation as an affirmation—made Patrick glance over at her.

"Hey, I was all the way in California," he said. "Just wait and see how often *you* race home once *you* go off to college."

Emma sat down beside him on the stoop, her bare legs crossed in front of her. "Annie was closer, though," she said, and it was a struggle to keep her voice light. "She was in DC all that time, and she only ever visited at Thanksgiving and Christmas. And Nate had a job then, with sick days and vacation days and no schoolwork, and he never came home either."

"That's what you get for being the baby," Patrick said, leaning into her with his shoulder. But when she didn't smile, his face fell too. "Come on, it wasn't so bad."

She shrugged. "You guys all had each other."

"And you had Mom and Dad," he said. "Still do, in fact."

"Lucky me," she said, and Patrick laughed.

"It's your great misfortune to have gotten stuck with an entire flock of odd ducks," he said with a grin. "But it could have been a lot worse."

"How?"

"We could have all been boring."

This time Emma couldn't help laughing. "Or stupid."

"Or *average*," Patrick said, widening his eyes.

"Hey," she said. "Don't knock average. That's my tribe."

"Nah," he said. "You're one of us. You just don't know it yet."

Emma looked at him sideways. "Why do you think they moved so much?" she asked. "Those years when I was little?"

She realized she was holding her breath as she waited for an answer, but she couldn't help it. Her parents had lived most of their lives in North Carolina, and had now spent the past eight years in upstate New York. They were the types who preferred to be settled for long periods of time, who liked to let their books accumulate a layer of dust. But just after Emma was born, they'd done short stints, first in Washington DC and then later in Manhattan, leaving each city after only a few years. The pattern had always struck her as odd, a restless spike of activity in an otherwise level existence. It was almost as if they'd been chased north somehow, and it had always seemed to Emma that there was something haunted in their flight. Only now she knew why. Now the ghost had a name. And a part of her suddenly wanted to hear Patrick say it.

"Don't know," he said, flicking his eyes away. "Change of scenery, I guess."

"It just seems kind of strange, them moving around so often like that."

He shrugged. "I suppose they had their reasons."

"So then why'd they finally stop?"

"Stop moving?" he asked, then smiled. "Because you told them to."

This, to Emma, didn't seem like an awful lot to go on. "So?"

"You don't remember?" Patrick said, looking off down the street, his eyes faraway. "You got first pick of rooms in the house upstate, since the rest of us were mostly gone at that point, and you walked straight up to the smallest one, the one with the twin beds . . ." His voice seemed to catch on the phrase, and he swallowed hard before continuing. ". . . And you pointed at it and said it was yours. That it felt like home. And when Mom and Dad asked you why, you said it was because you wouldn't get lonely there."

Emma tried hard not to let her face slip. "So?" she said again, though with less conviction this time.

Patrick turned to look at her, as if he only just now realized she was sitting beside him, and there was something in his eyes she hadn't seen before, something more genuine than the guy with the mind like a calculator, something sadder than the good-natured brother she'd always known. And somehow this was comforting. Somehow it made her feel just a little bit less alone.

He shook his head and then stood abruptly. "Nothing," he said, adopting his usual goofy grin, allowing the moment to be snuffed out as quickly as it had begun.

Overhead the sky had turned flat and gray, and the trees above them shuddered beneath the first curtain of rain. Emma held out her palm to catch the drops clinging to the fire escape above.

"We've already had forty inches of rain this year," Patrick said, hopping down a few steps, as if determined to return to his usual self. "That puts us ahead of the average by over ten inches. Do you realize that the volume of rain in Manhattan just for the month of June would be enough to fill—"

"Patrick," Emma said quietly, cutting him off.

"Sorry," he said, tipping his head back to squint at the sky. There was something about the way he was standing—the sun failing above him and the rain coming down fast now, the smell of the puddles and the cars splashing past—that slipped the heavy bolt of her memory, and Emma looked up at him through narrowed eyes.

"Do you remember that day in the park?" she asked, still trolling her mind for the details. "It was pouring, and nobody would take me, so I cried until you finally agreed."

Patrick looked at her from beneath wet eyelashes. "And we were the only people in the whole damn park."

"And we played in the puddles by the duck pond."

"And I tried to teach you about the ducks."

"But I wouldn't listen."

"Which just shows how far you've come," he teased, reaching out a hand to pull her up from the step. Her clothes were damp now, but there was something leisurely about the shower. A few people scurried past to duck into coffee shops or pubs, but neither of them seemed in much of a hurry to find shelter.

"See?" Patrick said, smiling at her as he started toward the corner. "I wasn't the *worst* brother in the world."

Emma hesitated for a moment before following him, thinking of her other brother, the one she'd never had the chance to know. She hadn't, until this moment, realized that she wouldn't tell Patrick about what she'd discovered in the attic. There was still too much she didn't understand, and it seemed as good a plan as any to act now and think later, to start moving in the right direction and save the questions for when she got there. She wasn't sure exactly how it happened, but suddenly the quest to uncover a secret had begun to feel like something secretive too.

Down the street a man with a trumpet began to play a bluesy song, and Emma closed her eyes to listen, the notes trembling out over the dampened block. When she opened them again, the sun was already beginning to split the clouds, and the world had gone from gray to silver.

"Ready to go?" Patrick asked, and Emma thought of the car parked uptown, of all the miles ahead of her, the many states and roads and possibilities, and she nodded.

She was ready.

chapter four

Cutting through the broad state of Pennsylvania, Peter couldn't help noticing the many green signs pointing off toward various colleges and universities. Some were bigger than others, some with fancy reputations, some he'd read about and some he hadn't. Growing up just down the street from a college, it was sometimes easy to forget there were so many others out there. He rarely managed to get much farther than the hilltop campus, where each autumn students from across the country filtered into the stately buildings, books in hand and ready to learn.

Peter had been waiting for years to join their ranks. Not there, of course, but somewhere like it, a place with an impressive name and a reputation to match. He felt he'd been ready to go off to school since at least the fifth grade, when he first saw an article about Harvard in the *New York Times* and swore to himself that he, too, would one day stroll across an unfamiliar campus, passing beneath ivy-covered arches in the company of thousands of other kids, all of them just as smart, just as odd, just as full of potential as Peter himself.

But he'd also known from a fairly young age that if he were to leave things up to his father, he'd probably end up at the community college a few towns over, getting lifts to class from the town's police force and clipping coupons for the rest of his life. Money had always been an issue for the Finnegans, a problem so constant that it had almost stopped seeming like a problem at all. It was just the way things were. But Peter was smart, and he knew it. And it was this—his ability to recite the first fifty digits of pi, to list all the countries of the world in alphabetical order, to calculate the square root of any number almost instantly—*all this*, he knew, was his ticket out of here.

But one night recently, when he'd first brought up the subject of applications over dinner, the sounds of the chapel bell ringing out from the campus just up the hill, he'd been shocked to discover that Dad actually hoped he'd choose to go *there*, of all places. It was true that the school had plenty to offer: history and philosophy, football games on October weekends, weathered stone buildings, and a national ranking high enough to suit Peter's lofty standards. But more important—and a fact not specifically mentioned in the glossy brochures—was that it was *right down the street*.

"It's just as good as the Ivy Leagues," Dad told him that night, arranging the pasta on his plate into a stringy volcano. It was one of those rare evenings when both his uniform and the TV were off, and he'd managed to assemble a dinner that didn't require the microwave. "And they offer a lot of scholarships for kids like you."

Peter narrowed his eyes at him across the table, but Dad seemed to be focused on his plate, pouring an additional helping of red sauce straight from the jar into the heart of the pasta volcano and then staring at it as if he expected an eruption. Peter couldn't help wondering if this was a punishment of some sort—this unforeseen effort to keep him close to home—or a cruel form of torture. Was Dad trying to put him in his place? Remind him of his roots? Be sure he knew that the socially challenged and motherless kid of a small town cop didn't belong at a place like Harvard or Princeton or Yale?

Because if he could get a scholarship here, couldn't he get one at any number of other schools? Places scattered across the country, in towns he'd never seen, states he'd never visited. It was no secret that he and his father barely understood each other, but it seemed hard to believe Dad actually thought that—given the choice—Peter would want to stay home for college.

The only thing harder to believe was that Dad even wanted him there in the first place.

Peter tried to imagine being the only one in the freshman dorms whose father was not an investment banker from Manhattan, or a doctor from LA, or a lawyer from Chicago, but the town sheriff, the one who might very well be responsible for arresting his new friends when they got drunk and went streaking into the mucky pond at the foot of the hill.

No, Peter had other plans, bigger plans. And they certainly didn't include ending up down the street from his dad and their dingy little house with its fading palette of greens and its smell of stale beer. He hadn't read every single book

31

by Charles Dickens or memorized the map coordinates of every state capital for nothing.

His dad, however, didn't seem to understand this, which is why Peter often preferred spending time with the Healys. Even though they both taught at the college, they'd also been professors at a handful of other universities, had moved around and seen the world before figuring out where they wanted to be. In fact sometimes he felt they understood him better than anyone—better than his father, and certainly better than Emma.

The first time he'd met the Healy family was just after they'd moved in, the summer that he and Emma both turned eight. Peter had fallen off his bike in front of their house, and Mr. Healy—who was perched on a stepladder in the openmouthed garage—rushed out to help him up. He led him in through the front door, a reassuring hand on the back of his neck, then disappeared to find the first-aid kit. Left alone in the coolness of the entryway, Peter bent to examine his knee. A moment later the professor returned with a Band-Aid, humming to himself.

"'Bearing the bandages, water and sponge, straight and swift to my wounded I go,'" he sang out, dabbing at the cut.

Peter recognized the words from a book about the songs and poems of the Civil War, a narrow volume he'd recently checked out from the library.

"Walt Whitman," he announced with a quiet authority, and the professor paused to look up at him, amused.

"Ah," he said with a grin. "A prodigy, huh?"

"No, sir," Peter said, shaking his head solemnly. "Just above average."

Mr. Healy seemed to find this funny, the entire barrel of

his chest shaking with a raspy, well-used sort of laughter, and once he'd smoothed the bandage into place, he stood and wiped tears from the corners of his eyes.

"Above average," he said. "Nothing wrong with that, don't you think?" This last part he directed over his shoulder, and Peter glanced up to see a girl sitting poised on the staircase, looking at him through the banister like a monkey at the zoo. She had long brown hair and the palest eyes he'd ever seen, a nearly colorless gray that settled on him lightly, and there was something in her manner—a casual lack of interest, a complete failure to be impressed by his knowledge—that made him wish he hadn't spoken in the first place.

Sometimes Peter felt like he'd spent the past eight years trying to dig himself out of that first moment they'd met, when he'd announced himself as someone intelligent to a girl who seemed to look upon this particular trait with great ambivalence.

But Emma wasn't like most kids who hated school or found homework boring; she wasn't indifferent and she wasn't stupid. It was as if somewhere along the way, she'd simply decided to take a different route than the rest of her family, a conscious decision that seemed to inform everything else in her life. Still, whatever it was that drove her to act this way—brilliant parents and intelligent siblings and a home that sometimes felt more like an old-fashioned literary salon than anything else—Peter couldn't help being jealous of the simple fact that these things *drove her* nonetheless.

Just the other day, on the Fourth of July, Peter had run into her as she made her annual escape from her family's cookout, this almost as much of a tradition as the party itself. He hadn't exactly been looking for her, but they had an uncanny habit of stumbling across each other nonetheless. Not that this was unwelcome. It was, in fact, the highlight of his days, when all the planning and mapping and waiting and hoping had been cast aside, and all he was left with was a town no bigger than a postage stamp, a father who barely noticed he was around, and a school he considered both too slow academically and too fast socially for someone of his nature. Emma's tolerance of him—he didn't fool himself into believing it was something it clearly wasn't—was the one bright spot in an otherwise dreadfully monotonous existence.

He'd fallen into step beside her as she headed up toward the campus, the collection of pale stone buildings and dorms set high above town. The sun had slipped to the other side of the valley, the day was cooling off already and Peter pushed at his glasses as he tried to think of something to say.

"How long's your brother in town?" he asked finally, and Emma looked over like she hadn't quite realized he was there until just that moment.

"Not long," she said. "I'm going back to New York with him tomorrow."

"Really?"

"Really," Emma said, then grinned. "He just doesn't know it yet."

Peter ducked his head and kicked at the tall grasses as they crossed the lawn. "Can I come too?"

She laughed, though he hadn't really been joking. "You don't even know how long I'll be away."

"I don't mind staying awhile."

Emma frowned and shook her head. "I'm not sure when

I'll be back. I'm probably going somewhere else after New York."

"Where?" Peter asked, quickening his pace to keep up with her, but she didn't seem to have an answer to this, or at least not one worth mentioning to him. "If there's no room, I could always take a car from the lot," he said, thinking of the small patch of asphalt behind their house that served as a makeshift lot for impounded or abandoned cars. "We could caravan."

"You wouldn't do that."

"I might," he said. "I know how to jump-start them."

Emma rolled her eyes, but Peter thought he could detect the faintest trace of interest even so. "Maybe another time," she said absently, already striding out ahead of him, her shadow long across the grass, leaving him there to watch her go.

The next morning, though he suspected she was already gone, he found himself standing in front of her house, wondering if it was okay to bother her parents so early on a Saturday. Much to his relief, the barbershop where he occupied himself five to six mornings a week for minimum wage was closed for the holiday weekend. It was a job he found nearly unbearable, pushing the broom in figure eights around the old-fashioned chairs, holding his breath against the fruity smell of the shampoo, and worst of all, disposing of the hair clippings, the flakes of dandruff still clinging to them determinedly.

Other summers, his jobs had been somewhat better. In fact, in his sixteen years in this town, Peter figured he'd done odd bits of work for at least three-quarters of the shops, everything from bussing tables and washing dishes to serving slices of pizza and bagging groceries. He'd once even worked as a janitorial assistant up at the college, which was just another reason he felt he could never go to school there: How could you attend classes at a place where you'd picked sludgy cigarette butts out of the fake plants in nearly every building on campus?

The lights appeared to be on in the Healys' kitchen, and so after a moment, he found himself following the flower-lined path up to their blue front door.

"This is a nice surprise," Professor Healy said, and his wife appeared in the doorway beside him, the two of them both dressed in khaki pants and navy sweaters, unwittingly matching in the way of long-married couples. "We're just about to have breakfast. You brave enough to try Katherine's eggs?"

Peter grinned. "That would be great."

He followed them into the dining room, and took a seat at the large oak table, which was seemingly engaged in a mighty struggle to stay upright beneath so many piles of papers and books. The surface was littered with reading glasses and pens, random pieces of day-old fruit and two mugs of coffee that had left permanent ring stains in the dark wood. He spotted a ruler and a calculator, sheaves of typed pages and others decorated liberally with red pen, and not for the first time, Peter wished that he lived in a place like this, a dust-filled room that smelled of books.

Mrs. Healy poured him a cup of tea, and Peter added some milk, watching the white liquid cloud his mug. Part of what he loved about coming here was this: the way they treated him like a colleague, a grown-up, a fellow intellectual. There were never any silly questions about school unless he brought up a certain paper he'd written or a subject he happened to be enjoying. He liked how they never assumed he was there to see Emma either; in their minds, it was just as likely he'd arrived for a discussion of the peculiar rituals of ancient Mayan funerals or the newest collection of poetry by Seamus Heaney.

There was something about them, too—an undercurrent of sadness, distant and lingering—that Peter found oddly comforting. He'd never had the chance to know his mother, and this absence often made him feel painfully alone. But every now and then—when Mr. Healy was scanning a bookshelf or Mrs. Healy's eyes drifted to the sunbleached windowsill—he could very nearly see it etched in their faces, a mystery that seemed both sad and sweet at the same time, like sleeping with a blanket even after you'd long outgrown it.

Now Mr. Healy passed Peter a section of the newspaper, and the two of them sat reading about the affairs of the world, weather that threatened to tip the globe off its delicate axis and wars that could shake the planet to dust.

"Well, it's nice to have *someone* around to appreciate my cooking," Mrs. Healy called out from the kitchen. "Since my own kids always seem so eager to escape."

Peter glanced at the doorway, where he could see her poking at the eggs on the stove. He was surprised by how easily she joked about this kind of thing, when just yesterday his own dad had accused him of more or less the same thing—trying to escape—only he'd done it with a look so dark and injured you would have thought Peter had suggested making a permanent move to New Guinea.

"I don't know about kids these days, Pete," Mr. Healy joked from behind his newspaper, his gray eyebrows bobbing up and down. "I mean, what kind of sixteen-year-old wants to spend a weekend in New York City? Must be terribly boring."

Peter looked up from his tea. "She's just gone for the weekend?"

He noticed the Healys exchange a brief glance, and once again, Peter felt his face flush, worried they might find another meaning in his question. This was not a subject Peter took lightly. He'd had time to give it plenty of thought over the years, and the conclusion he'd come to—one that he was determined not to think of as wishful thinking—was that he didn't like Emma. At least not in that way.

She was pretty, of course, with those unsettling gray eyes and that way she had of smiling with only one side of her mouth, and there was something careless about her that made the other guys at school glance at her sideways in the halls. But although Peter couldn't help being drawn to her, he chalked it up to more of a quiet affinity than a lovesick hopefulness. They were both loners in their own way—for Peter, out of necessity; for Emma, more of a choice—but he was fairly certain the bond they shared didn't amount to anything more than that.

He willed his face to return to its usual shade, a color pale enough to make his freckles stand out. "It's just that I thought she might be gone longer."

"Nope," Mrs. Healy said as she deposited two plates full of runny eggs onto the table, then snatched the newspaper from her husband's hands. "Back on Monday."

Peter realized that Emma must not have told her parents about the full extent of her plan either. It was his experience that people who lied were either hiding something or looking for something, and he wondered which was the case with her. He frowned at the eggs on his plate, then stabbed at one with his fork. There was far less confusion in things like math and history, with their straightforward numbers and dates. It seemed that people were a great deal more difficult to figure out.

chapter five

Emma was halfway to taking a bite of her burger—mouth open and breathing in the sharp smell of onions—when she caught a glimpse of something white streaking past the rest stop. She lowered her hands and looked off toward the straggly woods to her back, where a thin layer of trees separated the expressway from an office complex that lay just beyond. Seeing nothing, she turned her attention back to her burger, and she was just about to bite down again when a few of the kids from a nearby table began to scream and laugh and jump up and down.

It took a moment for Emma to realize it wasn't a wolf. Standing a few yards away in the grass and eyeing her burger with an unblinking gaze, a huge white dog was balancing on three legs. What had once been his fourth—the front right one—was now no more than a stump, cut short just above where the knee would have been. But there was something about the way he carried himself, like he didn't even know it was missing. He looked like a husky that had had a run-in with a bottle of bleach, pure white and enormous, but with a crust of mud along his belly and a collection of thorny brambles caught in his fur, which—along with the lack of a collar—gave him away as a stray.

He took a few hobbled steps forward, waving the stump of his leg up and down as if to say hello. Emma could see that one eye was brown and the other a startling shade of blue, as he sat down a few feet away from her and wagged his tail. Behind her a few people hastily shuffled their kids away or grabbed their trays and headed for another table. But Emma watched, fascinated, as he approached her.

She'd always loved dogs, but her parents had never allowed her to have one, and this, to Emma, seemed completely illogical: Wouldn't the best way to remedy irresponsibility be to have something to be responsible *for*? She'd spent years campaigning against the decision, dragging her parents down the street whenever she spotted a puppy, twice bringing home stray dogs (both of which were reclaimed within a few hours) and even once kidnapping the neighbor's puppy (also reclaimed within a few hours, though not quite as joyously).

And so now, as the white dog stood trembling a few feet away, his coat muddy and smelling of mulch, she held out one of her French fries. And when he took a tentative step forward, she tossed it in his direction, watching as he tipped his head back and caught it handily, snagging it in midair with a clean snap of his jaw. Each time she looked up from her burger, he had inched a bit closer, scooting along the pavement until he was settled near the end of the picnic table. And when he was near enough to rest his chin on her sandaled foot, Emma reached down and offered him another fry, which he took from her fingers with a well-mannered wag of his tail, his whole body wriggling with gratitude.

All her life Emma had dreamed of someday being a vet, even as her science grades continued their steady downward plunge. In fact she'd come so close to failing chemistry this year that her parents had forced her to have weekly tutoring sessions with Patrick, who spent hours rattling off formulas over the phone while Emma stared out her window, only half listening. Her grade had just barely improved—enough for her to pass the class, anyway—and her family was able to go on thinking of their youngest daughter as a scientific dunce.

But she knew there was more to being a vet than just science, even if her family didn't. Something about her shifted when she was around animals; she had a calming effect on them, a certain affinity that couldn't be learned from a textbook.

"It's not enough to think puppies are cute," Annie had told her. "There's a lot of science involved. And math."

"That's that subject with all the numbers," Patrick had pointed out, while Mom and Dad looked on with indulgent smiles.

Emma had always known she was different from her siblings, but that was the first time she'd felt it, really *felt* it, something sharp and sudden as a bee sting.

She'd grown used to being the token unexceptional one in a family of uncommon intellect, but sometimes it was an awfully lonely position. And though Emma was used to being on her own—may have even preferred it, in fact—she suspected this was only because it had become a habit, like anything else. It made her different from most kids her age, who clung to friendships like lifeboats, terrified of drifting too far. But Emma knew that if she were to allow someone into her life, then they might just discover what she secretly feared: that perhaps she was just as odd as the rest of her family, only without the brains to back it up.

The way she figured, it was okay for poets to be quirky. Professors are supposed to be absentminded, and geniuses are notorious loners. But Emma wasn't any of these things, and still she found herself easily distracted, prone to day-dreaming and wandering, with a habit of zoning out when anyone attempted to explain things to her. She hated directions and instructions and had little patience for studying. She was almost seventeen and had no real friends. She wasn't exactly normal, but she wasn't exactly *abnormal* enough either.

Lately she'd begun to wonder whether her twin brother would have been the same way. She liked to imagine that he might have been the sort of person to appreciate silly jokes and funny movies, the kinds of things that evoked blank stares from the rest of the family. He would have scoffed at science and laughed at math. He would have found poetry to be pretentious and confusing. He would have been her accomplice, her cohort, her partner in crime.

In fact, in the days since her discovery of the short and presumably tragic existence of Thomas Quinn Healy, Emma had begun to reflect on her life with the eye of a filmmaker. It was far easier than she might have expected to conjure up the brother she'd never known—a bit taller than herself, slightly less skinny, same dark hair and pale eyes—and she found herself simply adding him into all those places in her past where it had seemed something was missing.

Like the time Jimmy Winters gave her a bloody nose in the third grade. Emma had been in the process of explaining to him the difference between apes and humans—only very subtly implying that he might come closer to the former—when he knocked her cold on the wood chips. But if her brother had been there, standing at her side the way twin brothers do, she felt sure he would have stepped in between them, clocking Jimmy before he even had a chance to close his meaty little hand—opposable thumb and all—into a fist.

In much the same way, Thomas Quinn Healy—Tommy, for short—was now inserted into every family Christmas, every trial of summer camp, every day she'd endured alone in the school cafeteria, surrounded by the pretentious children of other professors or the too-rowdy kids belonging to the townies.

None of this was particularly difficult to imagine. The surprise wasn't how easily he fit into the gaps in her life. It was how naturally he took up residence there, quickly becoming a permanent fixture in her short history, a welcome revision of her past.

chapter six

There'd been an edge of static in the air as Peter walked home from the Healys' house after breakfast yesterday, that undercurrent of electricity that precedes summer storms. The sky had turned a sallow green in the distance, and the trees waved recklessly at the gathering winds. Peter kept his head low and his hands in his pockets, blinking away the bits of dust that were blown carelessly about. He paused at the end of his driveway, frowning at the squat and darkened house, then continued around it and toward the backyard.

Where a plot of grass should have been—a swing set or a barbecue, a basketball hoop or a bench—was instead a second driveway, a haphazard and bulging circle of asphalt like a tumor growing off the main one. There were three cars parked there at the moment, lined up neatly with their headlights pointing at the kitchen window like a cavalry awaiting charge. There was an ancient, rusted-out Chevy that had been there as long as Peter could remember, a maroon minivan his dad had recently impounded after it had been left for two weeks in front of the grocery store, and a blue Mustang convertible, not unlike the one he'd seen Emma drive off in just yesterday morning.

This one had shown up a couple of months ago, discovered on the side of the highway by some kids a few miles outside of town. Peter always wondered about the stories behind these abandoned cars, left like orphaned children on country roads. Most of the ones that came in were here on a more temporary basis—someone ran out of gas or collected one too many parking tickets, and the car was towed in to wait until its owner showed up to reclaim it—but the lengthier residents of this little parking lot always fascinated him. He imagined one day being the kind of person who was so accustomed to life on the road that leaving a car behind—to break up the monotony, to get a change of scenery, to hitch a ride and feel a different sort of vehicle surge beneath you—was just one more story to add to an ever-growing repertoire.

He walked past the minivan and toward the convertible, running a hand along its hood. The sky to the north had turned an angry purple now, and the air felt charged and ready. Peter looked over at the house, and the empty windows of the kitchen gazed back at him. He jiggled the handle on the convertible, but the door remained shut tight, and though he knew about the drawer full of keys in his dad's desk, he pulled his library card from his back pocket and slid it down into the groove between window and door—a move he'd learned from a book, though he doubted it would work on a more reliable car—and the lock sprang open.

Peter didn't have a car of his own. His driver's license, which he'd gotten just less than a year ago, was more or less decoration, permanently stuffed into the depths of his wallet. He'd learned to drive on his dad's squad car and had since seen very little of the road. But still, he liked to sit out here on certain gray afternoons, facing down the house and the sky as if in challenge, his foot poised above the gas pedal, his hands resting on the wheel, just a key turn away from motion and distance and velocity.

He sat down now on the scarred white leather of the driver's seat and closed the door as the rain started up, sweeping heavily over the car. Peter leaned his head back and closed his eyes and listened to the sound, like a thousand drummers attacking their instruments at once, but hollow and faraway and somehow comforting.

He'd always considered himself a wholly practical person, dependent on numbers and facts and statistics. But logical or not, there was something about sitting inside these motionless cars, these vehicles without destination or purpose, that always stilled his busy mind long enough for him to think about his mother.

Peter didn't wish for his life to be different in the far-reaching, deeply hopeful way that others often do, and he rarely imagined what things would be like if she were still alive. How could he? She was somewhere beyond his memory, a hypothetical answer to the rhetorical question of his life.

But his dad had never attempted to discuss her absence other than to occasionally announce—with a sense of resigned finality—that "bad things just happen sometimes." Even when he was very little, Peter had absorbed this information, had embraced it by the time he was five, hated it at seven, welcomed it again at ten, and rebelled against it at twelve. Now that he was nearly seventeen, it had become simply the statement it was: a chain of words that had dictated much of his father's life, and as a result his own.

He knew enough to realize that when she died giving birth to him all those years ago, a part of his father must have died as well. He understood this to be the way these things happen, the scripted etiquette of sudden death: the grieving widower, the crying baby, the rain falling across the freshly dug grave site. Peter had seen it a million times in the movies, but it bore such little resemblance to what was at stake now—to what amounted to his life—that he sometimes had trouble finding himself within the scenario.

Sometimes he was surprised that Dad didn't just come out and blame him for what had happened. Because even though he didn't actually say it, Peter could often feel it just the same. He knew his father loved him in his own way, but it was also like he couldn't bear to look at him sometimes, and Peter had felt the push and pull of this his whole life, of a dad who considered his presence both a blessing and a curse. It was like being on a roller coaster, pitched forward and then jerked back, ignored until he felt he barely existed in the house anymore, and then loved so fiercely and briefly it nearly took his breath away. It was like falling and falling and falling until the very last moment, when you were absolutely sure you'd hit the bottom, and then being swept upward again.

And so Peter could only ever manage to care about his dad with love measured in inches, slid forward and drawn back like an uncertain card player. It would be too easy to say *if things had been different* or *if she were still here* or *if he weren't the way he is*, because those things were immutable facts; nothing could make them otherwise. So he worried and observed; he thought too much and he moved too cautiously; he studied his father the way he did everything else, wishing things could be different.

Outside the car a peal of thunder made the ground tremble and the trees quake. Peter watched the raindrops slide down the windows, making streaky patterns on the stark canvas of the world just beyond, and he breathed in the musty smells of rain and dampness and old leather. He looked over at the empty passenger seat, the deep well that had been molded over the years by the unknown driver's copilot. It made him think of the way he'd often see mothers driving their kids around town, so cautious and careful, inching forward at intersections, wary of the car seats in back or the children buckled in beside them. And when they came to an abrupt stop—when a dog darted out into the road or a light changed unexpectedly—they never failed to fling an arm out to brace their kids, an instinctive measure of safety and concern for their charges.

Sometimes when he sat out here in the car, unprotected and exposed, Peter couldn't help feeling that way too. Like the weight of some invisible hand was keeping him safe.

He didn't even realize he'd been sleeping when he woke later to the drumbeat of rain on the windshield. But there was a new sound too, something louder, and when Peter finally blinked his eyes open, his heart stuttered in his chest. Someone was rapping knuckles against the hard glass of the window beside him, and a moment later the person bent at the waist to reveal the angry face of his dad.

"Inside," he said, his voice almost comically muffled from where Peter still sat inside the car, now fully awake. "*Now*."

Peter dropped his chin and fumbled with the door handle, and by the time he stepped outside and into the storm—which seemed to grow in intensity, a melodramatic prelude to whatever rebuke was sure to come his way—Dad had already disappeared into the house. Peter crossed the paved driveway, pulling uselessly at his collar as the water soaked straight through his shorts and T-shirt. He shoved open the back door and kicked off his soggy sandals, then stood dripping all over the welcome mat as three of Dad's poker buddies regarded him with interest.

"Baby's first carjacking," Officer Maron said with a grin, and beside him Lieutenant Mitchell—a pudgy man with an astonishingly large gap between his two front teeth—let out a low whistle.

"What a proud moment."

Peter ignored them and looked over at Dad, whose mouth was set in a thin line.

"It's not like I was taking it anywhere," he began, but Dad's left eye had started to twitch, which usually only happened when someone stole a stop sign or smashed the neighborhood pumpkins on Halloween. He grabbed a deck of cards and slammed them hard on the kitchen table.

"You boys set up," he said, his eyes still on Peter. "I'll be right back."

He stalked off toward the stairs, and the other three men looked at Peter sheepishly, averting their eyes and busying themselves with the poker chips as if suddenly embarrassed for him. Nobody liked to see someone stumble into the path of Sheriff Finnegan when his twitchy eye was acting up. Peter took a deep breath, then followed the heavy sound of Dad's footsteps.

He was in Peter's bedroom, of all places, his back to the door. He seemed to be deep in thought, contemplating the maps still spread out across much of the floor.

"Sometimes I just like to sit out there," Peter said to his dad's broad back, and he saw the muscles in his shoulders tense and then slacken again. "It's not like I was going anywhere. I didn't even have the keys."

"Exactly," Dad said, spinning around, fixing him with a hard look. "So answer me this: How does someone get into a locked car without keys?"

Peter pushed at his glasses and looked away. This was a famous tactic of Dad's, the pseudorhetorical question. It was far more effective than a simple accusation, in that it required an answer. And he had no problem waiting around until he got one.

"I was just *sitting*," Peter said, surprised to hear the resentment in his voice. "Is there a law against sitting these days?"

"In stolen property, yes."

Peter snorted. "It was hardly *stolen*."

"Whether or not you had intent to steal it is beside the point," Dad said, pacing a little circle around the room, the maps fluttering in his wake. "You were trespassing."

"Dad, come on," Peter said, suddenly weary. "Can't we just talk normally?"

His father raised an eyebrow. "Normally?"

"Without the cop jargon," he sighed. "You're off duty."

"Sure doesn't feel like it," Dad said. "Not when I come

home and find that my kid's broken into an impounded car."

"I wasn't—"

Dad cut him off. "I don't care," he said, his eyes flinty. He spread his palm over the globe on Peter's desk and then spun it hard. "If you want to run as far away as you can next year, then that's fine with me. But for now you're still living in *my* house."

Peter lifted his chin. There was hardly any point in arguing with Dad even when he was in the right—which was definitely not the case now that Peter's frequent break-ins had been discovered—but still, something in his throat felt tight, and the backs of his eyes were burning, and he couldn't explain the anger that gripped him except to wonder whether it had always been there and he just hadn't realized.

He knew, even before he said it, that it was a stupid thing to do. But he cleared his throat anyway. "It's my house too."

"Really?" Dad said, looking almost amused by this. "Because you sure as hell don't act like it. You can't wait to get out of here, turning your nose up at a good paying job and spending all your time over at the Healys, talking about books or whatever it is you do." His face was nearly white as he took a few steps closer, and for a brief and unreal moment Peter wondered if he might hit him. But then his voice grew quiet, and he straightened his shoulders. "Like this family isn't good enough for you."

Peter had always known this is what his father thought of him, but hearing him say it out loud was like being stopped short, like running up against a brick wall. It struck him for the first time ever that maybe his dad was actually *jealous* of the Healys, of what they meant to Peter, of what they represented. But instead of feeling sorry or sad, Peter only found himself getting angrier. Because what right did Dad have to be so resentful of the Healys' time with Peter, when he never showed the slightest bit of interest himself?

"I grew up in this town," Dad was saying now. "Your *mother* grew up in this town. She *loved* this place. And it's not good enough for *you?*"

He flicked a hand through the air as if to swat at a fly, but Peter just stood there, stunned and reeling. It felt like a betrayal of some kind, bringing up his mother in the midst of an argument like this, and it caught him completely off balance.

For as long as Peter could remember, Dad had held onto his grief with a silent and stoic determination, retaining a sorrowful monopoly on all those things that mattered, stories and memories and pictures. Because of this, Peter knew astonishingly little about his mother.

When he was younger, he used to make an effort, a kind of pitiful doggedness to his attempts. At dinner Dad would pass him a casserole dish of green beans, and Peter would immediately demand to know whether his mother had liked them.

"No," Dad would answer shortly, grabbing for the salt. The same held true for carrots and potatoes, chicken and steak, apples and bananas, until Peter began to wonder if his mom had eaten anything at all. If he were to believe his father, she didn't like sprinkles on her ice cream or dressing on her salad. She didn't like mittens or porches, Christmas trees or the ballet, teddy bears or fresh snow. Each of his questions was always punctuated by a short "no," and once he was old enough to understand that his mother probably *had* liked things like soap and flowers and socks—that his father's answers had simply become a habit, a reflex as rote as saying "bless you" after someone sneezes—he stopped asking altogether.

He couldn't help feeling sometimes like he wasn't entitled to the same kind of sadness as Dad, who had known her and loved her and laughed with her, who must have seen her make a sandwich and fly a kite and bite her fingernails and cry at the movies. He'd been witness to all those things that made her who she was, and he seemed to have decided somewhere along the way that all this was his alone to bear.

And so now all Peter could do was stare at him, angry that he'd invoked her name like that, sharply and carelessly, throwing it at Peter like a weapon he'd been storing away. It took him a moment to collect himself enough to respond.

"Then why do you even want me here?" he said eventually, before good sense could step in and give him a chance to turn around, to walk away, to keep his mouth shut. "If you really think that's how I am, then why do you try so hard to keep me here? Why do you make me feel so guilty about wanting to leave?"

Dad leaned against the desk and gave Peter a wounded look, causing him to falter and fall silent. When he spoke again, his words were quieter, more restrained.

"I'm here now, and we mostly just ignore each other anyway," Peter said, his face hot with guilt or regret or maybe both. "So what's the point?"

They stared at each other—each looking surprised to have stumbled into such foreign territory and found the other there too—and Peter thought to say more. But he wasn't sure what was left, and before he had a chance to do anything else, Dad lowered his head and scratched at the back of his neck and grunted. It was hard to tell if he was hurt or angry or upset, and Peter thought it was probably all of these things and more.

From downstairs they could hear Dad's buddies laughing loudly over something in the kitchen. Peter took a small step sideways, leaving the doorway clear, and without another word—without even looking at him—Dad walked straight past him and out of the room, moving heavily down the stairs.

As soon as he was gone, Peter sank down on his bed and rubbed his eyes. His back and shoulders ached as if they'd been throwing actual punches, not just verbal ones. He felt drained and exhausted, but also strangely relieved, like he'd been holding his breath for years and could now finally exhale.

Near his foot was a map of Gettysburg, and he looked down at the ridges and grooves running across the land. It wasn't just the nation that the war had divided; it was families, as well. Everyone had been fighting for what they thought was right, no matter who was on the opposite side of the line, whether it was your father or your brother or your son. It was about issues and causes and ideas, and what more could you ask of a person, Peter thought, than to risk all that they were for all they believed they could be?

Later that night, after the sounds of the poker game had grown quiet in the kitchen—the clinking of chips and shuffling of cards, the rowdy laughter and softer groans of failure when luck started to run out—Peter tiptoed down the stairs. He paused at the bottom and peeked around the corner to see all four men on the couches in the family room, their socked feet propped on the coffee table, an impressive display of empty beer cans arranged before them. From where he stood, Peter could only see the back of Dad's head, but despite the volume of the baseball game on TV, the others looked to be in various stages of sleep: one snoring, one with his eyes half closed, and the other with his mouth stretched open in an enormous yawn.

Peter slipped past the doorway and through the kitchen, moving silently around the table littered with stray cards and peanut shells and into the small hallway that bridged the kitchen and the garage, where he nudged open the door to his dad's office.

He could count the number of times he'd been in here: once when he'd been stung by a bee and rushed in without thinking; once when Dad forgot to bring some paperwork into the station and called to ask Peter to find it for him. Another time a rainstorm had caused the window to leak, and the two of them had worked to plug the hole together, keeping the water from ruining the many plaques and certificates that checkered the walls, tokens of appreciation from a town grateful for his dad's service.

Peter knew that one of the cabinets along the side of the room held two narrow shoeboxes filled with pictures of his mom. When he was little, he used to ask to look at them from time to time, and Dad would walk stiffly into the office while Peter hung back, clinging to the doorframe. He was always amazed at how gingerly Dad cradled the boxes, handling them with utmost care, as if they were important evidence in a criminal case rather than faded old snapshots.

Standing in the office now without permission, Peter felt nearly dizzy, and he moved quickly to the large oak desk in the middle of the room and pulled open the bottom drawer. There was a brown envelope that he'd seen before, the one where Dad dropped the keys each time a new car took up residence in the lot out back. He fished through until he found the set he remembered coming in months ago along with the blue convertible—an ugly blue rabbit's foot that had been dangling from the ignition that day like something that had curled up and died in the car—and he pulled them out and closed his hand around them.

It wasn't that he was necessarily going anywhere.

But it was nice to know he could.

chapter seven

Emma's life before this—first in North Carolina, then Washington, then New York City—was difficult to bring into focus. There were still the lingering outlines of houses and apartments, vague reminders of wallpaper patterns, a garage with a basketball hoop, a backyard with a swing set. But it was hard to separate what she knew from what she had seen in home videos and photo albums, from stories pried from unwilling memories.

Nobody in her family parted easily with information about the past. There were few tales of birthday parties or summer vacations unless they happened to coincide with a historical event, a book signing, or an academic conference. Her parents always teased Emma for her impatience—that skittish streak that kept her always on edge—but it was they who were hard to pin down. They had minds only for certain intellectual pursuits, and as she grew older, Emma saw that it was just getting worse. In a way it was not unlike a disease. Her dad was being slowly ravaged by poetry. Her mom had very nearly succumbed to the study of burial rites worldwide.

Somewhere along the way her family seemed to have come unglued; when, Emma wasn't exactly sure. But she was beginning to wonder whether it had more to do with her forgotten brother than the natural forces of distance and time.

When her cell phone began to ring—dancing along the planks of the rest stop picnic table—Emma looked up in surprise. A few feet away the dog was lying on the grass, looking hopeful about the appearance of more fries, and he pricked his ears forward and eyed the phone. Emma could see on the screen that it was her parents calling, and she suspected that Patrick had now spoken to them. He was probably furious with her, and though she knew she should pick up, she couldn't bring herself to do it, instead watching the phone until it fell silent again.

They'd be nearly frantic by now, she was sure, but she had no intention of turning back, so what good would it do anyway? It would only be a few more hours until she reached DC, and she could call them when she got to Annie's. By then she'd be nearly halfway to North Carolina, too far for them to object to her continuing on.

She stood to toss her garbage in one of the bins, giving the dog one more pat as she headed back over to the little blue car, which was now sandwiched between two campers in the parking lot. As she squeezed by the one wallpapered with Texas-themed bumper stickers, she was surprised to find the dog at her side. He sat back and thumped his tail against the pavement, his bad leg tucked up close to him, his head cocked first to one side, then the other.

"You trying to hitch a ride?" she asked, stepping around him. He sat there and watched as she closed the door, then jammed the keys into the ignition, turning them once, twice, and then again. But the engine refused to catch, and she sat in the quiet car and leaned her head back on the seat, telling herself not to panic. After a moment she tried again, and a thin trail of smoke rose from the seams of the hood. Emma stared at it, and then beyond, to where the dog was still watching her, his mouth hanging open in a great doggy smile, looking like he was very much amused by her current predicament.

"It's not funny," she said as she strode past him and back toward the building. He trotted after her, a white shadow beneath the high ball of the sun.

In her pocket the phone began to ring again, and Emma was about to hit ignore when she changed her mind. She waited until it had stopped—until her parents gave up for at least another few minutes—then scrolled down until she found a different number.

If she were to call Patrick, he would only yell at her about the car and demand that she turn back. Her parents would want to come pick her up, and Annie would wonder why she thought it was okay to show up unannounced in the first place. If she were to call a tow truck, they would only charge her far too much and then put her back out onto the road, where the car would probably break down again in another fifty miles or so.

But Emma was on her way, and she knew for sure that she couldn't stop now. And so she sat down at a picnic table and called the only person she could think to call.

Peter picked up on the first ring. "Hello?"

"Hi, it's Emma."

"Hey," he said, unable to hide his surprise. "How's the trip?"

"Okay so far," she said, and beside her the dog tilted his head as if to make the obvious point that the trip was not, in fact, okay so far.

"Good," he said. "Are you still in the city?"

"Not exactly."

"Where are you then?"

"In Jersey," she said, biting her lip. "Not far from Philly. You wouldn't still want to come along, would you?"

There was a long pause on the other end of the line, and Emma could almost hear Peter's mind at work. He had a way about him that might seem a bit odd to other people, but she'd grown used to it over the years. They'd known each other since her family first moved here when she was eight. Like her, Peter didn't have many friends at school. He seemed mostly to prefer his own company, though he'd always been different around Emma. She didn't think this could be called a friendship exactly, but she didn't necessarily mind having him around either. He spent nearly as much time at her house as she did, and it didn't escape her notice that, in many ways, he fit into her family far better. He knew everything there was to know about the Civil War, and had a tendency of bringing any subject around to it in the same way the rest of her family couldn't help letting their own specialties creep into everyday conversation. But he could also remain quiet for impressively long periods of time without feeling the need to say anything, and this suited Emma just fine.

"My car sort of died," she admitted. "But I'm not quite ready to turn back yet."

"Well, where are you planning on going?"

"North Carolina."

Emma held her breath as she waited for Peter to ask all the logical questions—*why?* and *where exactly?* and *for how long?*—but was surprised when he asked her something entirely different.

"Could we make a detour?"

"Where to?"

"Gettysburg."

"The *battlefield?*" She lifted her eyes to the sky, wondering if she'd made a mistake in calling Peter after all. *Gettysburg?* "That's got to be at least a few hours out of the way."

"I could always go on my own, then pick you up afterward," he suggested, and Emma looked around at the trucks rumbling in off the highway, the men with tall hats and heavy boots, the families eating French fries by the handful.

"No," she said a bit too quickly. She was already in enough trouble as it was, she thought. Might as well see some sights along the way. "Gettysburg sounds great."

Once they'd made the arrangements—an exchange of directions and landmarks and information—Emma left the dog behind and wandered back inside. It would be hours before Peter made it down here, and so she set about passing the time, losing a few quarters at the arcade, observing the flood of people from a bench beside a gumball machine, and leafing through magazines at the gift shop. There were rows upon rows of New Jersey souvenirs, glass thimbles with the state flag and spoons stamped with the official flower. There were coins and mugs and snow globes with the boardwalk underneath, the sand whirling beneath the glass like a snowstorm.

Emma ran a finger across a dusty pack of cards—each with a picture of one of the state's many so-called attractions—and wondered at the kind of people who collected these things. It was at moments like this one that she was grateful her family was so different. They might not watch stupid movies or care about who won the Super Bowl. They might not be able to get through dinner without bringing up a long-dead poet or famous mathematician, but they also didn't collect pens from different states. What they collected was far more important than that: words and stories, causes and facts. And it occurred now to Emma that perhaps her role in all this was to catch what they didn't, to find and preserve and hold on to the memories that had slipped from their grasp.

Before heading back outside, Emma stopped in the bathroom and stuffed her pockets with paper towels, then grabbed an empty soda cup and filled it with water. Out on the patio the dog was sprawled beneath the table she'd been sitting at earlier, and he scrambled out from under the bench to join her. He shied away at first when she tried to clean him up, gently untangling the burrs from his coat and dabbing at the dried mud, but soon enough he rested his head on her knee and let her continue. She picked the twigs from his fur, massaged the dirt from the pads of his paws, cleaned a small cut on his snout. Around them the parking lot continued to rearrange itself, the cars coming and going without pause, and the sun slipped lower in the sky, the shadows lengthening across the pavement. The dog let out a weary sigh, and Emma did too.

A few feet away a rectangular billboard advertised area events and attractions from behind a thick pane of yellowing plastic. The notices formed a border around a large map of Northern New Jersey, its colors muted by weather and time. Emma's eyes kept returning to the center of it, where a red circle with a tiny arrow jutting down like a spike of lightning announced YOU ARE HERE, and she couldn't help wishing it were always so easy to locate herself.

chapter eight

What Peter hadn't told Emma was that he was already on the road—shooting south toward Gettysburg as if he'd been summoned to battle there himself—and this alone should have struck him as a warning sign. If she knew that he'd already gone through the trouble of stealing a car and sneaking away from his dad, and not for her sake, not for any grand reason, but simply out of frustration at the latest in a long string of frustrations, then it wouldn't seem like such a very big deal that he was now on his way to rescue her.

And much to his surprise Peter found himself hoping that Emma would think it was just that. A very big deal.

He checked his phone one more time—just to be entirely, completely, utterly certain that the call had actually taken place—and felt a strange sense of excitement that made his stomach wobble and his hands flutter on the steering wheel. A smarter person would have told her that he couldn't come, would have stopped himself from getting off at the next exit, making a slight change in direction and heading east toward New Jersey. But although Peter was smart about a rather impressive range of things, dealing with girls was simply not one of them.

Up until Emma called, he'd been driving on sheer worry, propelled by a nervous fear of what Dad might do when he got off work later this evening to discover that both his son and the car were gone. Peter tried to distract himself by thinking of all the places he might now visit, the national parks and historical monuments he'd always wanted to see. But what if they weren't what he imagined? What if the battlefields were overrun by tourists? What if the Smoky Mountains weren't that much better than the hills of upstate New York? What if the World's Largest Ball of Twine didn't turn out to be very big at all?

Peter had never been much of a rule breaker or a boundary crosser, had rarely attempted to stick a toe over any sort of line, and he could blame Dad all he wanted for this. But a small part of him also knew that the reason he'd never ventured anywhere was because of the worry that the reality of the world wouldn't match up to his dreams.

Still, their argument yesterday had triggered something inside of him, and Peter had spent much of the night staring at the lacework of shadows across his ceiling, wakeful and restless. The keys to the blue convertible were tucked away in the toe of one of his sneakers, and he got up twice during the night to fish them out, turning over the cool metal in his hands, running a finger along the rabbit's foot as if testing his luck.

The thing was, he and Dad didn't usually fight. They

snapped at each other from time to time—they cast dirty looks and sighed with heavy, pointed sighs—but mostly they just kept their distance. So when Peter had padded down the stairs this morning, already stiff and awkward at the idea of their inevitable interaction, he wasn't surprised that Dad didn't even look up from the paper.

"Morning," he greeted him, and he saw Dad's left eye twitch, just slightly, though his gaze never wavered from the sports section. This was their usual way of dealing with things—to ignore them, to pretend they'd never happened, to forget about them and hope they might go away—and normally that was just fine with Peter. But as he poured himself a bowl of cereal, he realized for the first time how much the silence bothered him.

Last night hadn't been an argument over picking up his dirty socks or forgetting about what was in the oven so that the whole house smelled like a campfire. It hadn't even been about where he wanted to go to school next year. It had been much deeper than that. They'd talked about his mother—the rarest topic of all in a house where most topics went untouched—and the very mention of her should have warranted something more than this evasive shuffling of newspapers and clinking of cereal bowls.

And so Peter fixed a falsely bright smile on his face as he sat down. "Anything going on in the world?"

"The Mets lost to the Cubs," Dad grunted, not bothering to look up from the paper. This, of course, was a deliberate jab at Peter, a reminder of Dad's disappointment that his only son found sports to be pointless and boring (running in circles around some bases? tossing a ball into a hoop? grown men tackling each other on a muddy field?).

Normally, these attempts at conversation flickered out with the first sports reference of the morning, but today Peter beamed at Dad across the table. "Hope they can pull it together this season."

Dad raised his head to look at him with undisguised suspicion. "What're you trying to talk about baseball for?"

Peter shrugged. "What else would we talk about?"

"Look, if you're trying to make some kind of point—"

"I'm not trying to do anything other than talk."

"I'd think you were all talked out after last night," Dad said coldly, setting down the newspaper as he collected his plates. He dumped what was left of the mushy cereal into the garbage, then stood washing his dishes at the sink, his back to the table.

Peter cleared his throat, determined. "Last night you said that Mom—"

But Dad whirled around, spraying the room with soapy water. "Don't you know when to quit?" he said, his voice hard. "Just leave it already."

Peter took off his glasses, wiping away the flecks of soap with the end of his shirt. He was on the verge of losing his nerve, and wasn't entirely sure why he was still pressing the issue. He took a deep breath.

"You were saying how much Mom loved this town," he ventured again, the forced cheeriness now entirely gone from his voice. Because this was the thought that had kept him up last night. He'd known that they'd grown up here, that they'd met in high school and gone to prom together and been married in the chapel on the hill. But he didn't know any of the particulars, and hearing something other than a fact—that she was born this year and died that one—

had reminded him that she must have once taken walks here, picked flowers in the park, and said hello to neighbors on the street. It was a testament to how little he knew about her that it took something as mundane as this to send him vaulting into a past that didn't belong to him, fueled by curiosity and frustration and a desperate longing to shout when all he'd ever been allowed were a few timid whispers.

But Dad was looking at him now with such abject disbelief that Peter nearly brought a hand to his face to make sure nothing was growing there.

"Of *course* she loved it here," Dad said, and for a moment Peter thought maybe this was the beginning of something, that they'd sit back down together, lean across the milk-stained tablecloth, and have an actual discussion. But then Dad's left eye began to twitch again, and he brought a heavy hand down on the back of Peter's chair and lowered his face. "It was her home."

"Yeah, but—"

"She was smart," Dad said mildly, as if this quality weren't necessarily numbered among the things he missed about her. "Very smart."

Peter opened his mouth, but Dad scraped back a chair and sat down again across the table, giving him a long look.

"She didn't feel like she had to go running off to see the world," he said, bowing his head to examine the tablecloth. He used his fingernail to chip at a crusted piece of ketchup left over from last night's dinner. "Her life was here. She was happy *here*."

"It's not that I'm *un*happy here," Peter said quietly. "It's just that there are other things, other places . . ."

There was a long silence, interrupted only by the dripping

of the kitchen sink and the hum of the air-conditioning from the next room. Finally, Dad shook his head, frustrated, and stood up to leave. He tipped the contents of his coffee mug into the sink, tried twisting the faucet off again, then grabbed his sunglasses and hat from the counter. Peter watched all this with a sort of detached fascination, aware that something had shifted between them, an opening of something that perhaps should have been left closed.

Dad had a hand on the back door when he turned around once more. His eyes flicked across the room, taking in the drab green curtains and the faded floor tiles, the fraying tablecloth and his improbable son.

"She wasn't happy here *in spite* of being smart, you know," he said. "She was happy here *because* of it. She was smart enough to know a good thing."

"Then I guess she was smarter than I am," Peter said, his voice barely audible. The words emerged almost before he could think to stop them, and it was obvious by the way the door slammed that Dad had heard him loud and clear.

Later that morning, when Peter pulled the blue car out to the end of the driveway, his hands were shaking. He didn't know where he was going or what he was doing, only that it felt like it was already too late to take it back. And as he drove deeper into the state of New York—moving so quickly along the well-known map routes that it almost felt like falling—his mouth was dry and chalky with the very real fear that at any moment a police car would flip on its lights and peel out after him.

He knew that if it weren't for Emma, he probably wouldn't have made it very far. It simply wasn't in his nature, this tendency toward flight, this ability to break the rules without a second thought. No matter what he told himself, no matter how much he'd like to believe he'd have made it all the way to Gettysburg, in reality, he probably would have only stopped for pizza a few towns over, wandered to the farthest corners of the county, maybe waited until it was dark out before slinking back home to accept his punishment.

But then his phone had begun to ring, and the trip had suddenly changed from something meandering and lonely and spiteful into something more purposeful, an unlikely adventure with Emma, a journey filled with incredible possibilities. It was no longer just an afternoon jaunt. It was an expedition. It was a voyage.

It was unlike anything he'd ever done before.

All afternoon Peter tried not to imagine what Dad's reaction would be when he found out. After the first fifty miles he stuck a Post-it note over the clock on the dashboard, because all he could think about was the rapidly approaching hour when his father would arrive home from work to discover an empty house and a missing car. And it wasn't until five o' clock came and went, and the sky fell a shade darker, and the rest stop grew closer, and the phone in his pocket failed to ring, that Peter was struck with a new worry. That perhaps his dad *had* noticed that he wasn't there, and just didn't care enough to do anything about it.

But for the moment, at least, he was on his way, and he distracted himself by thinking about all the landmarks he'd always wanted to visit, not just the battlefields— which stretched up and down the coast like a scar across the land—but all the other things too: the Appalachian Trail and the Washington Monument, the Liberty Bell and the Smithsonian. In Pennsylvania alone there was the Hershey Museum (with its unimaginable amounts of chocolate) and the National Aviary (with its unending varieties of birds) and the town of Punxsutawney (home to the world's most famous groundhog). In Virginia he'd visit Colonial Williamsburg and Jamestown; South Carolina had the world's largest peach (an astounding one hundred and thirty-five feet tall and seventy-three feet wide), and Georgia had America's Smallest Church (which held only thirteen people). There was Disney World and Cape Canaveral, the wetlands and the Outer Banks, South of the Border and the Kennedy Space Center, and that was all just the East Coast.

But when he pulled into the rest area, a solitary patch of ugly concrete in northern New Jersey, and saw Emma sitting there—hunched on a picnic table beside a large white dog, her legs pulled up so that her chin rested on her bare knees, somehow managing to look bored and worried and excited all at once—Peter realized that this was even better.

chapter nine

Emma wasn't exactly sure what she'd been expecting—something more *Peter*, perhaps a minivan or a Volvo, something blocky and safe, a low-slung, sensible car with good mileage. So when the blue convertible came lurching up alongside the curb, she couldn't help laughing.

It was nearly the same as the other one—the one parked lifelessly across the lot—and Peter looked so comically out of place in it, his usually combed hair ruffled by the wind, his glasses speckled with bits of dirt, his arm slung over the passenger seat in a display of forced casualness.

"Hi," she said, and he grinned back at her somewhat less certainly, then looked down in surprise when the car gave a little jerk forward.

"Uh, let me just go park," he said, twisting his mouth in concentration as he fiddled with the gearshift. "I'll be right back."

Emma slid off the picnic table, and beside her the dog

leaped to his feet too. They eyed each other until Peter reappeared a few moments later, clutching the keys and looking somewhat sheepish.

"I didn't have much of a selection, and it seemed to run okay . . . ," he started to explain, throwing a hand in the general direction of the parking lot. The collar of his shirt was twisted and crumpled, and his shorts were too baggy for his skinny legs, and he was shifting from one foot to the other, clearly nervous about her or the car or the situation in general.

Emma attempted a reassuring smile. "It's perfect," she told him, because after nearly four hours here she would have been happy if he'd shown up driving a lawn mower. "Did you have any trouble getting it?"

"No," Peter said a bit too quickly. "None."

She nodded, and they stood for a moment in an uncomfortable silence, Emma only now really absorbing the idea of it: that she and Peter Finnegan were about to embark on a road trip together. She cleared her throat—to say what, she wasn't exactly sure—but before she could think of something, the dog limped over and bumped at the back of her leg, causing her knee to buckle. She swung her head around as he backed up a few steps, looking pleased with himself.

"Whose dog?" Peter asked, raising his eyebrows.

"Nobody's," she said. "He's been keeping me company."

Peter accepted this information the same way he did most everything else, without comment or judgment, only a thoughtful and unreadable nod of his head.

"Can we grab some food before we get going?" he asked, glancing over toward the hulking lodge of a building, and though Emma would have been just as happy to never set foot there again, she nodded and led the way.

"So what are you gonna do about your brother's car?" he asked, once they'd ordered and carried their trays back outside again. They were joined by the dog, who gazed expectantly at the food, following each fry like a spectator at a tennis match.

Emma took a sip of her milk shake. "Leave it here, I guess."

"Won't it get towed?"

"I doubt it," she said, not really knowing at all. "We shouldn't be gone much more than a week, and there are so many cars coming in and out of here."

He licked his fingers one at a time. "So then what happens in a week?"

"We'll get it repaired," she said with a shrug. "I don't know. We'll figure something out then."

Peter seemed pleased at the "we," and Emma realized she was too. It was a strange little crew she'd gathered— her slightly odd next-door neighbor and a three-legged dog—but it felt good to have company all the same.

"I saw your parents yesterday," Peter said, and Emma lowered her eyes. "It didn't seem like they realized you'd be gone for so long."

As if on cue her phone began to ring again, and she jammed her thumb against the off button. "You didn't say anything, did you?"

He shook his head. "My dad doesn't exactly know where I am either."

"Oh," Emma said, feeling worse instead of better. This only meant they'd have more people worried about them, more parents trying to figure out where they were. Peter's dad was a police officer—the town sheriff, of all things—and she wondered what kind of trouble two almost-seventeen-year-olds could get into for this kind of thing.

But Peter was now beaming at her from across the table, his eyes large against his freckled face—looking as desperate for approval as the dog at their feet—and so she smiled back at him with more confidence than she felt.

When he finished his burger, he balled up the wrapper to toss into the nearby garbage can. But his throw went wide, glancing off the side of the bin, and the dog pounced on it, bobbing his head up and down and looking confused when it didn't easily clear his throat. Before she had a chance to think better of it, Emma sprang up and wrestled him into a headlock. Ignoring Peter's protests, she pried open the dog's mouth and thrust a hand in, emerging triumphantly with the slobbery wrapper. The dog coughed a few times, and Peter stared at her.

"You shouldn't stick your hand into a strange dog's mouth," he said, sounding so much like her father that all Emma could do was nod wearily as she returned to her seat, the dog now pressed against her leg and eyeing her with a look of great devotion.

Peter regarded him skeptically. "He's not coming along, is he?"

"From what I've seen of your driving, I doubt he'd be up for it," she teased, and Peter turned as red as the dot of ketchup on the end of his nose.

But even so, Emma wasn't surprised when the dog trotted after them later, waiting patiently while Peter helped her check the engine of the car one more time. Once they were satisfied it was good and dead, she locked the door and they carried her things across the parking lot, moving from the old blue convertible to the new one. They climbed inside, and Peter put the top down, and then the dog—looking slightly miffed at not having been invited—took a running start and catapulted himself into the back, his toenails skittering across the trunk before he slid down into the seat.

Emma twisted around to look, and Peter stared at his rearview mirror in surprise. "Well," he said after a moment. "I guess he earned it."

The dog wagged his tail and rested his chin on the side of the car as they pulled out of the rest stop. The wind flattened his fur and made his nose twitch, and he closed his eyes, looking about as happy as Emma suddenly felt.

"I've always wanted a dog," she said. "I feel like every kid should have one."

"Maybe not one this big though," Peter said. "He could just about flatten someone with those paws."

"Nah," Emma said, reaching back to rub the dog's ears. "He's a gentle giant. I can tell."

"I hope you're right," he said with a grin. "And I hope he doesn't decide he'd like to eat us."

They drove on in silence for the first hour or so, heading west across Pennsylvania, moving fast along the tree-lined highways that sliced through rivers and ravines. Every so often Peter reached over and swiveled the gearshift in small baffling circles, like the joystick to some old video game, and the car staggered onward, the open top and rushing wind making it too loud to talk. Emma pulled on a sweatshirt and curled up in the seat, content to let herself be carried along by someone else for a change.

But even later, once they hit the back roads and the

breezes fell flat all around them, Peter remained quiet, and Emma began to fidget. She glanced over, watching him as he drove, his back straight and his eyes roving the horizon, where a pink band had formed above the bluish hills. A field of cows gazed back at her from the side of the road with vacant, dull-eyed stares, and Emma frowned back at them.

It was hard to understand Peter's lack of curiosity, of surprise, of *anything*. If the situation had been reversed, if *he'd* called from a rest stop in New Jersey and asked *her* to come get him—and not just to pick him up and take him home, but to drive on to North Carolina for no apparent reason—she wouldn't have hesitated to tell him he was out of his mind.

But Peter was different. Not only had he agreed to come get her, but he'd done so without requiring any sort of explanation, without questioning her reasons for the trip. And while it was true that this was pretty much how things had *always* been between them—Emma distant and unbothered, Peter quietly eager—it felt different now.

They'd known each other for eight whole years, had waved across their lawns and said good morning and occasionally walked to school together. They'd passed each other in the halls and nodded in the cafeteria and even once been lab partners in science class. Peter had eaten breakfast at their kitchen table more times than Emma could count, and while he talked with her parents, she'd passed him the butter and filled his water glass and teased him for getting jam on his face.

But the truth was, they'd rarely talked beyond the barest skeleton of a conversation—the hellos and how-are-yous and good-byes that serve as the tent poles of common decency—and somehow that had never struck her as particularly odd. You wouldn't be expected to tell your deepest secrets to the mailman, and you would never think to confide in the checkout guy at the grocery store. It was the same thing with Peter Finnegan. He was the guy next door. The nice-enough boy from her school. The smartest kid in her math class. Nothing more.

But it was different now. At home the silence between them was comfortable, something worn and familiar. But here in the car there was a sharpness to it, as if the air itself had turned into something prickly. And for reasons she couldn't quite explain, Emma felt that this was somehow her fault.

"Don't you think this is sort of weird?" she asked abruptly, and she watched as his eyes flicked from the gauges to the gas pedal to the rearview mirror, the dog drooling in the backseat. When Peter seemed satisfied that there was nothing especially weird about any of these, he shrugged.

"Weird how?"

Emma shook her head, trying to ignore the dog panting heavily near her right ear. "Aren't you wondering why I'm dragging you to North Carolina with me?"

"You're not dragging me," he said simply. "I don't mind."

"That's not the point," she said. "Don't you want to know what we're doing?"

"I thought maybe you wanted to visit your brother."

"Yeah, but come *on*," she said. "I could've taken a plane."

He pushed his glasses up farther on his nose. "Road trips are fun."

"Yeah, but by yourself?"

"You don't ever seem especially desperate for company," he pointed out. "And anyway, now there's two of us."

Emma relented, absently tapping her fingers on the windowsill. Maybe it was better this way, that she didn't tell him about her brother. When she tried to imagine what she'd even say, it always came out sounding weirder than it was. Or maybe it was just that it *was* weird. Regardless, it seemed there was no good way to tell someone you were taking them to visit your dead brother's grave.

"Well," she said after a moment, "aren't you at least curious why I didn't tell my parents?"

He hesitated, then shrugged. "You didn't ask why I didn't tell my dad, either."

This was true, of course; she'd been too wrapped up in her own concerns to inquire after Peter's. For all their differences Emma could see they were similar in many ways: self-sufficient, if lonely; independent, if a little lost. And though it seemed to her that the air was still thick with unasked questions, she gave in to the silence. It wouldn't be the worst thing, she figured, getting through the trip in this way. Even two different trains on two different tracks could reach the same destination, as long as they kept moving.

chapter ten

Peter Finnegan didn't have a whole lot of experience with being wrong. But as he drove along Route 194 toward Gettysburg, he was becoming increasingly aware that he'd been mistaken about at least one very important thing.

Somewhere in the last hour or so he'd come to the conclusion—somewhat miserably—that he did, in fact, like Emma Healy.

Quite a lot, as it turned out.

She was sitting beside him with one knee propped against the door, her elbow resting on the windowsill, her long hair tied back into a messy ponytail. Every so often she slid her eyes in his direction and gave her head a meaningful little shake, and he knew she was puzzled by his silence on a growing number of topics.

It wasn't that Peter wasn't curious. The truth was, he was dying to know the reasons behind her insistence on getting down to North Carolina, her strange determination to make this trip. But he also didn't want to seem overeager; lately, when it came to Emma, he had a tendency of opening his mouth with the intention of saying something intelligent, only to find, at the very last minute, that it had turned into something outrageously stupid instead.

He was already fairly certain that he'd had a sesame seed stuck in his teeth the whole time they'd been talking at the rest stop, and now he couldn't help obsessively searching the inside of his mouth with his tongue, so he was sure he must look like an underfed camel. Even worse, it had taken him at least half an hour to wipe his nose and find that he had ketchup streaked across the back of his hand. He hoped Emma hadn't noticed, but it was a bleak and unlikely hope; unless you were a clown or a highly unusual reindeer, it was hard not to stand out with a red nose.

To add to all this the convertible had turned out to be moody and erratic, lurching this way and that like a skittish horse. Peter's shoulders were tense and his neck was stiff from attempting to wrangle it into a generally forward-moving direction, the car wrenching testily beneath them every few miles. As they slowed at an exit, the brakes made a grinding noise, and a smell like rotten fruit or overripe socks drifted up from the backseat, where the dog—looking appropriately mortified—crawled to the other side to avoid his own stench. Peter glanced in the rearview, and Emma wrinkled her nose and laughed.

"Jeez, Peter," she joked. "At least warn me next time."

"Funny," he said stiffly, too nervous to manage a laugh.

Emma snaked an arm between the seats and plucked one of his maps from the floor in the back. It snapped in the wind as they sped up again, easing onto the expressway, and she examined it with a little frown of concentration. But just as quickly, she seemed to lose interest, and Peter gritted his teeth as he watched her attempt to refold it, making a mess of things as she crumpled the paper along the wrong lines.

"I don't need the maps," he told her. "I know where we're going."

"Then why do you have so many?"

He opened his mouth to answer but had no idea how to explain. Emma tossed the one she was holding onto the floor, then twisted to grab another, tugging a European atlas from beneath the dog, who resettled himself unhappily on an underwater survey of the Pacific Ocean.

"It's really okay," Peter said weakly. "I don't need a navigator . . ."

"I don't mind," she said, running a finger between Germany and France.

Peter stifled a groan, turning his attention back to the road and hoping she couldn't tell just how flustered he was, his mind crowded with worries. He wondered if the car smelled funny, or if the engine was supposed to sound like something was being chewed up inside of it. He wondered if policemen were able to send out nationwide alerts for wandering teens in stolen convertibles. He wondered if Emma was worried too.

She hadn't been acting any differently than she usually did around him, disinterested and then excited in turns, abruptly short with him and then a moment later charming and engaged. Half the time she was so exasperating that Peter wished the car had an ejection seat, and at other times he found himself sneaking sideways glances at her, devolving into sappy daydreams about what it might be like to sling an arm over her shoulder as they drove.

When her phone began to ring again, Emma set the map down, and Peter tried not to wince as the edge caught the gearshift, neatly ripping Iceland in half. She bit her lip and studied the screen before once again deciding to ignore it, and Peter had a brief urge to reach over and answer it himself, not because he wanted the trip to end—not by a long shot—but because he felt a strange allegiance to the Healys. Somehow, this whole thing felt like more of a betrayal of them, who had always treated him like an adult, than his father, who had never failed to make Peter feel out of place.

His own phone hadn't made a sound since he'd set off from home earlier, and he wasn't sure exactly how he felt about that. He wondered if his dad might have spoken to the Healys by now; though they weren't much better off in the information category, they at least had somewhat of an idea of Emma's whereabouts, based on the fact that she'd been with Patrick until this morning. Still, Peter didn't like to imagine what might be going through Dad's head right now. He wondered if it was an angry silence or a careless silence, this thing between them. He wasn't sure he wanted to know.

But it was nearly dark now, the domed sky closing in all around them, and he had a foot on the gas pedal and two hands on the steering wheel, he had Emma Healy beside him and a strange dog in the backseat, and he was heading to Gettysburg, a place he'd been fascinated with since he was eight years old and was first told about the unfathomable tragedies of that long-ago war.

Everything else was beginning to seem faraway and unimportant.

The dog turned in three cramped circles in the backseat, then settled down with his nose tucked beneath a paw, and Peter felt a quick rush of affection for him, a fellow outcast, as unlikely a stowaway as himself on this trip that nobody really understood.

Emma leaned forward to turn on the radio, then fiddled with the dial, landing on each station for a minute or so before flipping through to the next one. When she caught Peter looking at her with raised eyebrows, she shrugged and switched it off again.

"Maybe we should play a car game or something," she suggested.

"Like what?"

"I don't know. The license plate game?"

"What's that?"

"You try to spot as many license plates from as many different states as you can," she explained. "You'd probably love it. It's very 'fun with geography.'"

"Sounds slow."

"So is geography."

He made a face at her. "What else you got?"

"The animal game?"

"Let me guess," he said. "See how many animals you can spot?"

Emma grinned. "Sheep are worth two points each."

"Thank God we're not in Ireland," he said. "Where do you come up with these anyway?"

"They're pretty standard road trip games," she said.

"What happened, you were too busy with the atlas as a kid to have any fun in the car?"

"Sitting in the backseat of a police car like a criminal isn't exactly fun."

Emma laughed. "You could build up a lot of street cred that way."

"Yeah, I looked like a regular thug with my bowl haircut and glasses."

"Who would've thought you'd turn into an *actual* criminal all these years later?"

He knew she was joking, but Peter felt suddenly nervous anyway, adjusting his hands on the wheel and glancing up at the rearview mirror as if he were expecting someone to be tailing them.

Emma looked down at her lap. "My birthday's next week, you know," she said, and Peter glanced over at her, trying to compose his face in a way that might suggest that this was news to him, although he knew—had always known— just exactly when her birthday was, despite the fact that his was only a few days later and she unfailingly missed it every year.

"I wanted it to be different this year."

"Different from what?"

She shrugged. "My family's not great with birthdays."

Peter thought of *his* past birthdays, the well-intentioned gifts his dad always gave him—baseball cards or action figures or a skateboard—which were always so perfectly and completely wrong, and no matter how hard he tried to pretend otherwise, the day always left them both with a sour taste in their mouths.

"My family's just . . . ," Emma was saying, her face small

and pale against the rest of the world as it scrolled past. "They just never manage to get things quite right, I guess."

"Most don't," Peter said shortly.

"Yeah, but my family's different."

He set his mouth in a thin line. "Most are."

They rode in silence for a few miles, easing off onto quieter roads, the car moving purposefully through the deepening dark. The barest sliver of a bone-white moon had already appeared low in the pale sky, and a fog hung at knee level in the fields. As they reached the top of a sloping hill, they could see the lights of the town of Gettysburg glowing white in the pocket of a valley. Emma leaned forward and blinked out at the town, but Peter was more interested in the shadowy areas that bordered it, the wheat fields and orchards and pastures that had once been the stage for so many important battles.

"So, I guess that's sort of the reason for the trip."

"Your birthday?" Peter asked, but even as he did, and even as she looked away, he suspected there were many reasons—not just a restlessness that he, too, could understand, but also a search for something bigger, something that maybe not even Emma yet understood—and for now, the rest didn't need to be put into words.

chapter eleven

The moment they stepped out of the car, the dog began turning in small, pitiful circles, flattening his ears and pausing every now and then to cast a doleful glance in their direction. Peter didn't seem to notice; he stood with his back to the car, the keys in one hand as he stared out over the ink-black patchwork of fields. But when the dog let out a low whine, Emma thought that maybe she understood: There was something about this place, an eerie stillness, an almost tangible feeling that something irreversible had been stitched across the land, and it made her shiver too.

"Ready?" Peter asked, turning to her with a faint smile, and Emma nodded, not entirely sure what she was agreeing to. There was nobody else around. All the tourists had returned to their hotels. The employees who spent their days going through the motions of those blood-soaked skirmishes had long since hung up their uniforms and retreated to the bars in town, and the local kids had surrendered their playground to the muffled hour just before dusk.

But Peter was already half trotting down a steep hill and toward the fields that broke off from the road, and even the dog—who'd been hanging back uncertainly—now went streaking out ahead of him with that uneven three-legged gait of his, a white blur in the darkness.

"You can't see much," Emma ventured, her voice made thin by the wind. She skidded down the damp grass in her flip-flops, narrowly avoiding a rabbit hole. "Sure you wouldn't rather just come back in the morning?"

Peter was waiting at the bottom of the hill. "We can do that, too."

"Super," Emma managed. From what she could make out, they were standing in a valley bordered by shadowy ridges that looked like great sleeping monsters in the dark. For a moment she was calmed by the thought that this could be anywhere—any old meadow in any old town, the kind of place where dogs run in circles and kids fly kites and flowers grow each spring—but then a face seemed to materialize out of the fog, a metal statue of a soldier gazing impassively over the site of his own death, his horse frozen beneath him, his gun forever at the ready.

"Are you sure we should be here?" Emma asked, and when her words were met with only a heavy silence, she turned to see that Peter had paused before the statue. His head was bent over the plaque, and it struck her as somehow impolite to bother him now, like interrupting someone at a funeral, so solemn was the look on his face, reverent and humbled at once. The dog had circled back and now sat rigidly at her side, his mismatched eyes darting between the pale stone monuments and the rows of cannons that formed an uneven line across the field.

Emma watched Peter's back, the rise and fall of his shoulders, wondering and worrying, trying to guess how much of these desolate grounds he'd want to see tonight, how far into the past he'd be tempted to wander. There were other things too: She wondered where they would sleep later on, and how far it was to Washington. She wondered if her parents were still calling the phone she'd left in the car, whether Patrick would ever speak to her again, what they would do with the dog when they got to Annie's. All these worries seemed to expand in the darkness, until Emma felt nearly short of breath, and she tried not to fidget as she waited for Peter to finish whatever it was he was doing.

After a moment he turned around, his face pale in the dark. "Isn't it . . . ," he began, then trailed off, apparently unable to find the right word. Emma could think of several that might fit the bill—"creepy," "depressing," "morbid"— but she didn't say any of them.

"This part's called East Cemetery Hill," he said quietly, waving his hand in a circle. "And over there was Culp's Hill, where the Union formed their fish-hook line."

Emma raised her eyebrows. "Fish hook?"

"It was named for the shape of their defense," he told her, then whistled for the dog as they began walking again. Through the trees she could see splintered headlights as they neared the road and whatever lay beyond, and their feet made loud crunching noises in the dirt. Peter held a tree branch for her as she ducked beneath it, her foot getting snagged on a twisted root. There was a wooden fence strung out along the length of the two-lane road, and Emma squinted to make out a run-down farmhouse and a few crooked trees on the other side of it.

"Lincoln made his address just up there," Peter said, already looking awestruck as they waited for a truck to lumber past, then jogged across together. "It's one of the most famous speeches—"

Emma snorted, and Peter glanced back at her, his eyebrows raised.

"Give me a little credit," she said indignantly. "I might not know a lot, but I *do* know about the Gettysburg Address."

He grinned. "Okay, then."

As they walked deeper into the woods, he told her about battle formations and casualties, unexpected victories and retreats; he brought the whole messy past lurching into the present with newfound significance. And much to her surprise Emma found herself listening as he spoke, as he took a field like any other and turned it into a story, tracing for her a history that had happened on the very spot they were standing.

"So why do you care so much about this stuff?" she asked, the question settling heavily between them. It was clear she'd interrupted Peter in some sort of reverie; he shook his head as if remembering himself and his whereabouts, then turned to her and blinked. Emma cleared her throat. "I guess it just seems sort of random," she said. "I mean, why the Civil War?"

"It's not really about the war," he said softly. They were at the edge of another field now. The moon had slipped behind a bank of clouds, and though he was standing just feet away from her, it was hard to make out his face. "It's not even about any of the issues really, slavery or the Union or any of the other stuff that kept it going for so long."

"So what, then?"

He shrugged. "It's about seeing something get put back together again, I guess. Especially after coming so close to falling apart. I mean, if a whole country can bounce back from something like that, then it sort of seems like anything's possible."

Emma breathed in, tilting her head back to look up at the sky, where the stars were punching holes in the endless darkness. Beside her the dog turned circles in the grass, and the wind died so suddenly it was as if the world had stopped breathing.

"Peter," she said quietly, so quietly it took a moment for him to face her, with an expectant look that nearly made her change her mind. But his words were still rattling through her head, and the night had grown still, and she could almost feel the secret she'd been carrying struggling to work its way out of her. "There's something I haven't told you."

He grinned at her. "You're secretly a Civil War enthusiast?"

"No," she said. "I once had a twin brother."

His face changed, slipping just slightly, but his eyes remained steady on hers. "Once?"

"I found a birth certificate in our attic," she said. "Just last week. But there was a death certificate, too. From a couple days later."

Peter lowered his chin, and Emma watched him carefully, trying to make out what he was thinking. His brow was furrowed, and he was staring at the ground so intensely that he might have been calculating the number of blades of grass in the field.

It struck her then, as it had so many times before, that his way of seeing the world must make life fairly difficult. When he looked at a house, it was like he could only ever see a network of pipes and beams, as if the rest of it—all the little details that made it what it was, the furniture and family photos, the chipping paint and sagging ceiling—were hardly there at all. It was like he saw deeper into things than most people, an explorer winding his way into the tiniest corners of a cave, while Emma, on the other hand, seemed to always see her way *around* things, skirting the edges of whatever lay in front of her, the interesting and the extraordinary as much as the mundane and the dull.

She'd always had a worrying ability to see right past everything.

"I'm really sorry," Peter said finally, his jaw set as he turned away, keeping to the dirt path that wound toward a distant grove of trees. Emma hurried to catch up to him.

"That's it?"

"What else is there?"

She frowned. "You could at least say it like you mean it."

"I do mean it," he said without pausing. "It's a terrible thing."

"Well, aren't you curious about why they never told me?" she asked, stopping abruptly in the middle of the path. It took him a moment to notice she'd fallen behind, and when he did, he spun around with his eyebrows raised high above the rim of his glasses. They remained there like that for a few beats too long, squared off and uncertain, each nearly lost to the darkness.

"I'm sure they had their reasons," he said eventually.

"Well, I want to know what they were," she said. "I

mean, maybe something really bad happened. Maybe there was an accident or something, or someone wasn't watching him carefully enough, and—"

"Emma," Peter said, cutting her off, a look on his face that fell halfway between sympathy and impatience. "This isn't a movie. Bad things just happen sometimes."

She was struck by the sound of his voice, so full of reproach. After a moment he turned to start walking again, his head bowed and his arms held stiffly at his sides.

"That's it?" she called after him. "*That's* your answer? Bad things just happen sometimes?" She shook her head, then pushed past him, plunging farther down the path on her own. "That's not good enough. At least not for me."

She could hear his footsteps on the dry ground, the snap of twigs as he followed her. She wasn't sure whether he had an answer for that, whether he'd planned to respond, because before either could say anything more, they broke through the band of trees and stumbled out into a clearing. Emma stared at the sight before her, rings of gravestones like crop formations rising from the wine-colored shadows. There were rows upon rows of unmarked headstones fanning out in half-moon shapes, tiling the manicured lawn.

"What *is* this?" she whispered, following Peter between the lines of pale stones, which spiraled outward like veins across the bruised and broken land. The whole ghostly formation centered around a looming monument, the white marble bright in the dark, and it was here that Peter paused. After a moment Emma realized that he was speaking, his voice low and his head bent, murmuring almost unconsciously.

She moved closer, standing just beside him, so that their shoulders were nearly touching as they tilted their heads to look up at the monument.

"Peter?" she asked, but he didn't look at her.

"Lincoln's address," he said, without any trace of embarrassment. "This is about where he made it."

Emma nodded, falling quiet again to let him continue, listening as he chanted the words as if in prayer. And when he finished, she closed her eyes.

"'The world will little note,'" she said softly. "I like that line."

Peter nodded. "'The world will little note,'" he repeated, "'nor long remember what we say here.'"

"They thought it would be just a footnote," she said, thinking how they couldn't have possibly known, those soldiers buried beneath this very ground. They couldn't have realized that this speech, this battle, this particular moment would live on so powerfully. It had refused to stay a footnote. It had refused to be forgotten.

Peter swept an arm across the cemetery. "Some people say it's haunted."

"You believe in that sort of thing?"

"Not really," he said with a little shrug. He seemed about to say something more, then changed his mind, turning to start the walk back. But Emma stood where she was, suddenly reminded of another cemetery—the ending point to this trip—and of her brother, who had been buried there after only two short days in the world. Emma rubbed her hands together, suddenly cold. She closed her eyes, and it was almost as if he were there beside her, not a ghost or a memory, but just a feeling of great comfort, like she suddenly had at her side the one person in the world who would ever understand her.

She smiled, letting her eyelids flutter open again, but when she turned to look, it was not her brother—neither real nor imagined—but Peter who was standing just inches away from her, lost in thought and smiling, too.

chapter twelve

When he pulled into the parking lot of the diner, Peter turned off the engine and reached for the door handle without looking at Emma, since he already felt certain he could guess the look on her face. There was a blinking neon sign that read SID'S DINER in orange letters and below that declared that what appeared to be the hollowed-out shell of an old barn was THE SCRUMPTIOUS CIVIL WAR SENSATION.

It didn't look like much of a sensation from the outside, where only one other car was parked in the gravel lot, a faded blue pickup truck with a rusted shovel in the back. But Peter could see inside the windows to where the walls were plastered with old wartime flags and posters and a few old muskets hung above the counter. It was like the worst of all theme restaurants. Like Medieval Times, he thought, only without the jousting. And probably not quite as cool, if such things could ever really be considered cool in the first place.

But Emma—who had been uncharacteristically quiet during the walk back from the cemetery—didn't seem to mind. They left the dog to poke at the garbage bins outside and then walked in to find themselves set adrift somewhere between 1860 and 1960, the room alternating between actual antiques from the Civil War and outdated furniture from when the diner must have first opened. There were only two other customers, a pair of men hunched low over their steaming mugs of coffee as they scraped the crusted dirt from their boots onto the metal legs of the stools.

Peter and Emma slid into an orange vinyl booth and sat examining the menu and the ketchup bottle and the dirty silverware, making fans and tubes and tiny squares out of their napkins rather than speaking to each other. Peter's eyes roamed the walls, the framed declarations and tattered flags, the Union caps and Confederate slogans, and he thought of explaining their significance to Emma, but he wasn't sure this was the best way to break the silence.

Once they'd ordered from a bored-looking waitress—Custer's Custard Pie for Peter and Abolitionist Apple Strudel for Emma—they resumed their own separate investigations of the cutlery, playing with forks and spoons, inspecting the edges of the table and the tears in the seat where the yellow stuffing bloomed. Peter could very nearly feel it, the way the space had suddenly expanded between them. He didn't have much practice with this kind of thing, but the trip ahead—four more states and five hundred more miles—was beginning to seem far longer than it had at first.

"So," Emma said finally, more like a sigh than a word. It was the first time either of them had spoken since they'd ordered, and they both seemed slightly unhinged by the sound of it.

"So," Peter said back. He was aware this was perhaps not the world's most brilliant response, but he wasn't sure exactly what the moment called for; it wasn't like Emma to look this way, weary and overwhelmed and just a little bit sad, sitting in the orange light of the diner in front of her half-eaten plate of dessert.

She looked up at him, her eyes wide and serious. "Do you think this was a mistake?"

"The apple strudel?"

"No," she said, but he was pleased to see a hint of a smile. "The trip."

He shook his head.

"You're not ready to turn back then?"

"Not unless you are."

"Okay, then," she said with a nod, though she still looked a bit uncertain, and Peter could understand why: After all, they had nowhere to sleep tonight and were no doubt in a world of trouble with their parents. They were somewhere in the middle of Pennsylvania, and in many ways it had all stopped seeming like a game.

It had all started in the cemetery, of course, when she'd turned to him as if expecting someone else, her eyes widening just slightly, her face going abruptly pale. Gettysburg was supposedly one of the most haunted places in the world, with frequent sightings of ghosts in the trees, cameras inexplicably jamming when people tried to take photographs, glimpses of women in white and all manner of wandering spirits. But Peter knew that not all ghosts wore white sheets and roamed through cemeteries; there were other ways of being surprised by the past, and he suspected Emma had been thinking about the brother she'd never had the chance to know, and this was something he could understand too.

But she wasn't the only one who was unsettled by the evening. Peter also found himself troubled by the thought of the dead brother they were chasing down the coast, though he knew his reasons were somewhat more selfish.

All these years he'd taken such pride in his acceptance by the Healys, who seemed to find him endlessly interesting, engaging in a way his own father never recognized. But now he was wondering whether there'd been more to it than that. He couldn't help thinking that maybe he reminded them of the son they'd never had the chance to know, that maybe that was the only reason they ever asked him over, or set an extra place for him at the dinner table. And this gave him a funny feeling, a wobbling in his stomach, like a joke that had gone over his head.

He glanced up at Emma, who was still intent on her food, and he thought of her family, of the way Mr. Healy collected certain books for when he knew Peter was coming over, and how Mrs. Healy always made him a mug of hot chocolate to sip while they discussed the famine ships or the Boer War or the Indian removal. He thought of the way he felt so at home there, the way he seemed to belong, as welcome as if he'd been a part of the family himself.

And it occurred to him that maybe, just maybe, he'd been using them for the exact same reason they'd been using him.

When they finished eating and filed back outside, they were pleased to find that the dog was still there to greet them, apparently having nowhere better to go either. He wiggled from head to toe when Emma spilled the contents of a napkin—half her apple strudel and the crust of Peter's pie—onto the ground for him. The air was thick with fireflies making lazy circles, dipping in and out of the pools of light from the diner, which transformed them from floating lights back into winged, black insects.

Emma hoisted herself up onto the trunk with an expectant look in his direction, but Peter had noticed a phone booth just outside the diner and was already walking back over. It took him a few tries to jimmy open the door, which was rusted along the top, and the inside smelled like a litter box. Aware that Emma was watching from just outside, he dug in his pocket for a few coins and then dialed his number at home.

He let the phone ring twice, his heart skipping around, but before his dad could pick up, Peter slammed the receiver into its cradle and walked back outside.

Emma raised her eyebrows at him, but he only shrugged.

"So what now?" she asked, letting her legs dangle against the bumper of the car. Maybe it was the darkness, or the heaviness of the food in their stomachs, or the chill that had crept into the air without them noticing. But the trip now had a fragile feel to it, gone from sunglasses and milk shakes and the wind on their faces to this: the two of them staring at each other in the back lot of an old diner, unsure of their next move and uneasy about all the ones that had come before this.

"Are you gonna want to see more of this stuff in the morning?" Emma asked, and Peter tightened his jaw, trying to ignore the tiniest bubble of irritation that had risen up in his throat. Just an hour ago she'd been interested and engaged, asking questions about the history of the place, genuinely fascinated by his knowledge of it. But now she'd once again grown tired of it all, and Peter was mad at himself more than anything for feeling wrong-footed and surprised, when he should have known better by now.

He wondered if there was a rule that you had to love *all* of someone, or whether you could pick out only the best parts, like piling your plate full of desserts at a buffet table and leaving the vegetables to go cold in their little metal bins.

He frowned at her. "This *stuff?*"

"Gettysburg," Emma said, waving a hand in the general direction from which they'd come. "Have you seen enough, or are we doing round two in the morning?"

"I wouldn't mind seeing the reenactments tomorrow," he said. "But we wouldn't have to stay long."

"What should we do about tonight, then?" she asked, sliding down off the trunk. The dog was rolling in the grass at the edge of the parking lot, and as they stood there, the bell on the door of the diner rang out, and the two men emerged. They passed by the blue convertible with a nod, then drove off in the pickup truck, the tires spraying gravel at their feet. A moment later the waitress followed, locking up the door without acknowledging them and then taking off down the shadowy road on foot.

Peter and Emma exchanged a look.

"We could stay here," he said.

"In the car?"

He shrugged. "Got any better ideas?"

Emma regarded the convertible with some degree of doubt, but she climbed in anyway, and Peter followed, starting the engine and pulling it around to the back of the barn, where he eased the top up, the stars above disappearing bit by bit until there was only canvas left overhead. They didn't bother with pajamas or toothbrushes, instead eating the mints they'd taken on the way out of the diner and rummaging through the trunk for articles of clothing that might double as pillows. Neither said much as Peter wedged himself uncomfortably between the steering wheel and the gearshift up front and Emma curled up in the backseat with a map of Florida for a blanket.

Outside on the grass the dog snuffled and dreamed, his three good legs giving chase to some imaginary foe, but it took Peter a long time to fall asleep. He knew that he talked in his sleep, that he had a habit —according to his dad—of reciting coordinates at night, pinpointing random spots on the globe with a sort of dreamy accuracy. And so now he blinked at the worn roof of the car and watched the stars grow brighter on the other side of the windshield, listening to Emma's breathing even out, waiting for her to be the first to give in to sleep.

They woke in the morning to the sun peering intently through the windows, both of them stiff and sore and cranky. Peter's cheek was stuck to the white leather seat, and he banged his knee on the steering wheel when he tried to sit up, rubbing his sore neck.

"Morning," he said, glancing at Emma through the rearview mirror, and she gazed back at him with puffy eyes, her hair mussed and her eyes still caked with sleep.

He stepped outside to grab a clean T-shirt, sidestepping the enthusiastic greeting of the oversized dog, who pushed a wet nose into Peter's hand, looking for food. Somewhat reluctantly, Peter left Emma with the car to herself so she could change, and headed back over to the pay phone. He let the phone ring three times this time, hung up just as he thought he heard an answer, and headed back into the diner.

There was a rack of tourist brochures just inside—pamphlets advertising everything from haunted battlefield tours to historic B&Bs—and Peter stood counting what money he still had, thumbing through the bills and pushing the change around in his palm as if the coins might be convinced to pair up and multiply. He was fairly certain he'd be facing a cashflow problem within the next couple of days, but there was nothing to be done about it now, and so he bought three blueberry muffins from the same waitress as last night, then walked back outside and handed one to Emma and the other to the dog, who finished the whole thing in one go.

Emma had put the top down on the car, and she was now perched on the back of it, her feet planted on the seat where she'd slept. She'd never been one of those girls who worried much about her appearance—she spent most of her summers in flip-flops and a jean skirt, alternating among an assortment of faded T-shirts—but there was something even more rumpled about her this morning, her long hair uncombed and tangled, her cheek still bearing the lines from where it had been pressed against the seat last night.

"What?" she asked through a mouthful of muffin, and Peter blushed and ducked his head, realizing he'd been staring at her.

"Nothing," he muttered, reaching for a few of the maps, then folding them into neat squares, just for something to do. "Almost ready?"

"Sure," she said with a grin. "Wouldn't want to miss Halloween at Gettysburg."

"It's not like they're playing dress-up," Peter pointed out. "It's a *reenactment*. They recreate all the famous battles from the war."

"O-kay," she said, raising her eyebrows.

"That came from the Civil War, actually," he said, though he knew that now would have probably been a good time to come up with something less obviously nerdy as a follow-up.

"What did?" Emma asked, looking at him blankly.

"The word 'okay,'" Peter said with a sigh. It was hopeless; if his conversation starters tended to stray toward unsolicited Civil War trivia while at home in upstate New York, he figured he was pretty much a lost cause in Gettysburg. "When the troops returned from battle and there were no casualties, they would post a sign that said, 'Zero Killed.'" He traced out the letters in the dirt at his feet. "Get it?" he asked, glancing up at her. "Zero, K. OK. Okay."

"Right," Emma said, swinging her legs around the side of the car and climbing into the front seat. "I guess we should probably get going, then."

Peter slid into the driver's seat beside her and turned over the engine with the key, the blue rabbit's foot still dangling from the chain. They drove past the field where they'd stood the night before and toward the visitors' center, where they left the convertible in a lot with cars from a dozen different states, a rainbow of license plates and people with accents to match, all of them fanning out across the park with their cameras ready. Emma tried to coax the dog out of the car, but he was dozing comfortably in back, so they left the top down in case he changed his mind.

Everything looked different in the daylight. Without the early moon and the pale fog, the battlefields seemed to have shed their mystery, and something of last night's magic had been lost. But still, as he led Emma over the wedges of grass that ran alongside the road, Peter felt elated at being here. He grabbed her hand—just for a moment—as they were shunted through a gated entrance, then let go again once they made it to the other side. If it bothered her, she didn't say anything, and this was enough to make Peter feel like skipping the rest of the way.

Around them the stubbled land was marked off by plaques and signs that explained to visitors what had happened here on a long ago July day not unlike this one. But Peter already knew all they said and more. He looked around at the people with their noses tucked in brochures and guidebooks, and those trailing, sheeplike, after tour guides and park employees. He was used to feeling somewhat out of place most everywhere he went—at school or the barbershop, even at home—but here, where he knew everything, all the names and dates and facts, he somehow seemed to fit, and the knowledge of this welled up inside of him. It was like he'd been born a blue flower in a field full of red ones and had only now been plunked down in a meadow so blue it might as well have been the ocean.

"I used to have all these little army figurines when I was little," he told Emma as they wound past a group of European tourists who seemed deeply unimpressed by the empty orchards and fields. "The carpet in my room always had a thousand little footprints in it, which drove my dad nuts."

"What'd you do?" she asked absently, as they followed the signs toward where the reenactment would take place. "Play war?"

"Sort of," he said, trying not to notice as she checked her watch. "I had all these books about the battles, and I'd line them up in all the famous formations, and have them hold down all the hills and sites."

By the time they arrived at the Wheatfield, the reenactment had already started, and there were cannons going off like fireworks, setting shapeless clouds of smoke drifting through the burnt air. Emma rose onto her tiptoes and scanned the field.

"Blue's on the left; gray's on the right," she said, and then tripped along after him as Peter headed left toward the Union side.

"So, do people actually do this for a living?" she asked, squinting to catch a glimpse of the angled muskets and improvised movements of the actors, who were dressed in what looked like the uniforms of the day, careworn and muddy.

"I don't know," he said. "Maybe."

"Don't you think it's kind of a weird job? For grown men to be playing war for a living?"

Peter didn't bother answering. Around him there were kids cheering at the sharp crack of the guns, adults grimacing at the reminders of an ugly past, and Emma, shifting from one foot to the other, her interest clearly waning. The day was sticky and humid, and those who'd come here with the best of intentions now looked as if they'd much prefer a swimming pool to the unshaded remains of a former battlefield.

But as he stood and watched the lines shifting on the distant hills, the troops folding in and then back out of formations he knew by heart, it felt to Peter like remembering something he'd never really known in the first place. It was a part of each of them, this battle that had taken place for the soul of the country. The world was built upon fallen soldiers and ill-conceived wars, and this was one that had defined them all.

Unlike most people Peter didn't look to the future for reassurance; he understood that the only thing certain in life is the past. History repeats itself again and again, and every story has been told before. It seemed to him that life could be terribly unoriginal in that way, and the only manner of certainty—the only way to know what might be ahead—was to look back on what had already happened. You could always count on someone else having lived through worse than you, and this particular story—the Civil War, the best and worst of a whole country—gave him a firm sense of hope that anything and everything could be repaired. Even the worst struggles could end in reunion.

Now he couldn't help smiling as he watched the space between the two regiments on the battlefield, the tall blades of wheat leaning sideways, tickled by the wind.

"When they fought here," he said, "the whirlpools from the breezes made it hard for the soldiers to see, because of all the tides and eddies in the fields."

Emma was standing just beside him, and she lifted her chin in the first half of a nod. On the field the soldiers were now charging, barreling toward one another, brandishing guns and blades and flags, the horses of the higher ranking officers leaving clouds of dust in their wake.

"This was a huge turning point," Peter said. "All these battles."

"Hmm," Emma murmured absently, glancing up here and there when a mock explosion rippled through the crowd in gasps of surprise and delight.

"It rained on the last day," Peter said, pressing on with a sort of pathetic determination, a faltering resolve to try one more time. "There was a huge storm that evening, after three full days of the bloodiest battle the country has ever seen." He paused and looked reverently out over the land. "That's something, don't you think? How it kind of washed everything away?"

Emma peered up at the sky, which was turning a deepening shade of gray. "If we don't get going soon, we might have a storm of our own."

Peter sighed, and he took a few steps in the direction of the parking lot before Emma jogged over to catch up with him, appearing at his elbow with a look of confusion.

"I didn't mean *right* now," she said, falling into step beside him, and he shrugged, hoping his face didn't look as injured as he felt by her lack of interest. She bit her lip. "I didn't mean to make you—"

"Yeah," he said quietly. "You did."

She didn't seem to have much to say to this, tucking her hands in the back pockets of her jean skirt, her elbows jutting out like wings from her sides.

Peter shook his head. "How come you're always in such a rush?"

"I don't know," she said, then changed her mind. "I'm not."

"You are."

She opened her mouth to dispute this, then closed it again. They walked the rest of the way to the car in silence, and it wasn't until he'd started the engine and pulled out of the parking lot that Peter finally spoke again.

"Well, thanks, I guess."

"For what?"

"For putting up with that. I've always wanted to see it."

Emma looked up in surprise. "You'd never been?"

He shook his head.

"But I thought—"

"Nope."

"You knew where everything was," she said. "I mean, I just assumed . . ."

"I've read a lot of books," he said shortly. "I find it interesting."

At the entrance to the highway, he turned toward the signs for Philadelphia. The dog stuck his head between the seats, looking from one to the other like a kid whose parents have been arguing. Ahead of them the sky had begun to lighten again.

"It's pretty cool, the way you know so much about all that stuff," Emma said eventually, and Peter looked over, aware that this was her way of apologizing. "I'd never have the patience for it."

"For what?"

"Learning all the facts and dates and details," she said. "Caring enough about the past to bring it to life like that."

Peter smiled in spite of himself. "I thought that's what you were doing."

"What do you mean?"

"With your own family."

"Not really. It's not exactly like I'm—"

"But you are," he told her. "Like it or not, you're kind of a historian too."

chapter thirteen

The day she turned seven, an entire conference room of world-renowned anthropologists sang "Happy Birthday" to her in a hotel in San Diego. The foremost expert on Native American culture gave her an arrowhead, and the keynote speaker—a man so old the whole podium shook beneath his hands—asked whether she wanted to come up and help him with his speech.

She didn't.

For her tenth birthday Emma's parents threw her a small dinner party at home, where she—the guest of honor—was the youngest one by at least thirty years. The dean of the college spilled wine on her party dress, and the conversation quickly turned to the role of birthday wishes in traditional fairy tales. After she blew the candles out from atop an organic carrot cake, a biology professor leaned over and asked Emma what she'd wished for.

She pretended not to hear him.

All she'd ever wanted was a normal birthday, with a swimming pool or a magic show, a big-nosed clown twisting balloons into dogs, cupcakes with sugary frosting, and ice cream melting on plastic plates. But most years the big day was instead colored by gifts like maps and bug boxes, puzzles and history books, things she was told she'd come to appreciate someday, though as the years ticked by and the pile of unused presents in her closet multiplied, Emma began to seriously doubt that that day would ever come.

But now her seventeenth birthday was just four days away, and here she was hurtling toward North Carolina, carried south along I-270 by Peter Finnegan and his stolen blue convertible. And in a rare display of all those things that had so far eluded her in life—determination and persistence and dogged curiosity—she was secretly hoping to spend her birthday on her own terms, at the resting place of the person who'd once shared it with her.

They were well into Maryland when Emma took charge of the music, switching off the jazz station Peter had found and popping in a CD instead. After listening to the same song four times in a row, Peter leaned forward and jabbed at the stop button.

"Hey," Emma said, reaching to turn it back on.

"How can you listen to the same thing over and over again?"

She shrugged. "I'll probably listen to it a thousand times in a row, then never play it again."

He shook his head. "You're nuts."

"Nuts is a relative term in my family."

Peter turned off the expressway, and the road quickly

tapered off into a single lane, which wound through great swaths of farmland, the fields quartered off into neat slices of brown and green.

"Are we lost?" Emma asked, reaching for one of the many maps that wallpapered the back of the car. The dog was sitting squarely on top of the pile and looked greatly put out when forced to scoot over.

"We're fine," Peter said. "It's just nice to get off the highway now and then."

Emma frowned over the tangle of squiggles and lines on the map, trying to locate their whereabouts amid an alphabet soup of stars and dots and unfamiliar names. "How do you know where you're going?"

"I just do," Peter said, obviously pleased with himself as they left behind the billboards and gas stations for a series of small towns with white churches and general stores and vegetable stands.

"Okay then, Columbus," Emma said, tossing the map behind her again.

"Columbus got lost, actually," Peter said. "So not the best example."

"And you think *I'm* nuts."

"You are," he told her. "But it's not such a bad thing. Some of the most interesting people I know are a little bit nuts."

"Like my family?"

Peter rubbed a hand over his jaw and gave a little laugh. "They're not as strange as you think they are," he said. "They're *interesting*. There's a difference."

Emma shrugged. "Whatever."

"Maybe you're not looking hard enough," he said. "Besides, have you ever thought maybe you're just as interesting as they are?"

"I'm not," she told him flatly.

"I don't know," Peter said. "I think maybe it's too soon to tell."

They stopped for lunch at a seafood stand with checkered tablecloths and menus shaped like giant lobster claws. They were far enough from the coast, but the air still smelled salty, and the other customers were all laughing over their lunches. Emma leaned forward with her elbows on the table and smiled.

"What?" Peter said, looking at her suspiciously. She didn't blame him. Only this morning she'd been about ready to leave him in Gettysburg, but now the heat of the day had burned off and the dust had drifted away. In the past twenty-four hours the car had broken down and she'd somehow managed to pick up a stowaway dog and an unlikely partner in crime. But here they were, sitting in Maryland with the sun on their faces and the smell of seafood thick in the air; they'd made it this far, and suddenly that was all that seemed to matter.

"Nothing," Emma said, still grinning from behind her menu.

After they ordered, they watched the other customers cracking the tough shells of the lobsters and letting the juice run down their bare arms as they ate. Peter pulled a map from his back pocket and spread it out on the table between them, smoothing the creases along the wooden slats.

"So, I found a map of the town where Nate lives," he

said. "The one where you were born. And where I assume we're headed."

"Where?"

He looked up at her blankly. "In North Carolina."

"No, I mean where'd you manage to find a map of it?"

"Oh," he said. "In the trunk. Anyway, did you know there are three different cemeteries there?"

Emma shook her head.

"Do you know which one it is?"

She bit her lip, but said nothing. She simply hadn't thought that far ahead yet.

"That's okay, I'm sure Nate will know," he said. Emma must have looked stricken at this—the thought of having to explain herself to her family—because Peter reached over and quickly spun the map so it was facing her. "Or you can just close your eyes and point, and we'll go to whichever's closest."

She smiled at him gratefully, clapped a hand over her eyes, and jabbed a finger at the map. When she looked up again, Peter was marking the spot with a pen, humming over the grids in cheerful concentration.

"Okay, then," he said after a moment. "At least we know where we're headed now."

The dog began to squirm beneath the table, eyeing a little boy who was picking at a piece of corn bread. There was a small grocery store beside the restaurant, and Peter walked over to see whether they carried dog food. He came back a few minutes later carrying a small bag of kibble, which he poured onto a paper plate and set on the ground. But the dog only sniffed at it, then went back to eyeing the bread, and when their corn bread came, Emma passed her portion underneath the table.

"He's gotten spoiled," Peter said, kicking at the bag of dog food. "Or else he has no clue what it is."

Emma licked the crumbs from her hand. "Maybe he's just got good taste. We'll try again at Annie's house."

"Will she be okay with us bringing him?"

"I don't know if she'll even be okay with *us*," Emma said, forcing a laugh.

"Right," said Peter, but he looked nervous.

"It'll be fine," she told him, though she wasn't really sure. She hadn't seen Annie since Christmas, when she'd brought home her boyfriend, Charles, a political analyst for the *Washington Post*. He'd seemed mildly horrified by the chaos that reigned in the Healy household, which only grew worse during the holidays. He'd since moved into Annie's apartment, and Emma wasn't all that certain he'd appreciate his girlfriend's kid sister dropping by with her buddy the Civil War aficionado and the three-legged mutt they'd picked up at a Jersey rest stop.

"Have you ever been before?" Emma asked him, leaning back as the waiter set down their plates and trying not to meet the eye of the lobster on hers.

"To DC?" he asked, grabbing the butter. "Nope."

"Where *have* you been?"

"New York City."

"That's it?"

"That's it," he said.

Emma studied his face as he bent over his lobster, working his fork to split the shell with the expertise of a chef. There was so much she didn't know about him. They'd grown up next door to each other, but she'd never even been inside his house. He'd come over to hers, of course, but then so had the whole town. Their front door was always open, and there was a constant stream of people filtering inside to join them, whether for a family dinner or a fireside discussion about the plight of polar bears in the Arctic Circle.

But Peter had a tendency to hang back, always unnervingly quiet when she was around. Her parents seemed to think he was talkative and engaging, but Emma thought it was possible that she'd heard him speak more in the last twenty-four hours than in all the previous years she'd known him. It wasn't that he was shy, necessarily. He just seemed to be always measuring out his words, thinking before he spoke in a way that Emma couldn't ever manage.

Growing up, he'd always been nothing more than the kid from next door, the one who wore glasses and had a funny haircut and whose pants were always a couple of inches too short. But Emma was realizing now that Peter was the kind of person who tended to get overlooked. He was unfailingly patient and genuinely polite, but he was also surprisingly confident, capable and dependable and utterly sure of himself, and she was suddenly grateful to have him along with her. Because it's exactly these sorts of people—the ones who everyone's always underestimating—that you want at your side when you're running away from home, or driving the length of the country, or feeling somewhat confused as to your own illogical intentions.

"My dad was never big on family vacations," Peter was saying now, half hidden by the tablecloth as he smuggled his share of corn bread to the hungry dog.

Emma tilted her head. "My parents weren't either."

"But you've been everywhere."

"I've been to lots of colleges," she corrected him. "Lots

of universities and lecture halls and conference rooms."

"I can't wait to get to places like those."

"We *live* in a place like that."

"Yeah, but it's different. I mean, don't you want to go away for school?"

She shrugged. "My parents get free tuition there. And it's not like I'd get in anywhere better, you know?"

"But don't you want a choice? It's a great school if you're into history or literature or sociology. But what if you wanted to be a doctor or something?"

"I'm sorry," Emma said, laughing. "Have we met?"

"You could be a doctor if you wanted."

"Well, it's lucky I don't, then," she said, glancing down at the dog beneath the table. She thought of her family and their books, the way everything came so naturally to them. "I'm awful at science."

Peter set down his fork. "All I'm saying is that you shouldn't limit yourself."

"What about you, then?" she asked, eager to shift the focus from her and her academic failings. "Off to see the world? College in London? Masters in Paris?"

Peter smiled. "Wouldn't that be nice."

"And more trips to Gettysburg, of course."

"Of course."

"I can't believe your dad never took you there before."

"Yeah, well, he's not such a big fan of reenactments either," he said, and she noticed that he looked over— almost unconsciously—at a phone booth set just off the parking lot. "It's not like we never did *anything*, though. He used to take me fishing sometimes. We never caught much, so I'd always bring a book, and he'd get annoyed at me for

119

reading. Great father-son bonding time, those trips."

"Well, you do read a *lot*," Emma teased, and he threw his napkin at her.

"It's not like it would kill *you* to pick up a book every once in a while."

"You sound exactly like my parents," she said, wrinkling her nose at him. But Peter only smiled, his ears turning as red as the half-eaten lobster on his plate.

chapter fourteen

They'd barely gotten back on the highway when Emma began to tease him for driving like an old woman. There had been a faint hint of rain in the air after lunch, and so the top of the convertible was now up, and Peter felt hunched and slightly claustrophobic beneath it, his eyes trained on the road.

"What happened to the guy who tore into the rest stop?" she asked, propping her feet up on the dashboard and reaching over her shoulder to hand the dog a potato chip. "You were a maniac yesterday. Now I'll bet we get pulled over for going too slow."

Peter raised his foot with the intention of hitting the gas, but then saw yet another police car—this one tucked in the entrance of a fast-food restaurant just off the highway—and instead jammed down on the brake, causing the car to balk and both him and Emma to lurch forward in their seats. Behind them a truck driver leaned hard on his horn before swinging into the left lane and blowing past them in a haze of exhaust.

As they crawled past the dust-coated police car—a Maryland state trooper whose head was tipped back against the seat as he slept, his mouth propped open so that he looked a bit like a baby bird—Peter breathed out and loosened his grip on the steering wheel. It was nearly impossible to stop his heart from pounding each time they passed one, not necessarily because he was speeding or driving any more erratically than usual, or even because one of the taillights was cracked and refused to light up—though that last was also true. Mostly it was because Peter had started to see the face of his dad behind every shadowy windshield of every single emergency vehicle they passed.

Peter knew it wouldn't have been terribly hard for him to put out some kind of alert, the kind of thing that would come over every crackling radio in every worn-down cop car from upstate New York straight down to the very tip of Florida, a warning to every fellow man in uniform that the son of a sheriff had stolen an impounded car and was now fleeing to who-knew-where. Peter guessed it wouldn't take a whole lot of effort for his dad to call in a few favors, have someone fetch the blue convertible and reel them back home like a couple of squirmy fish on a hook.

But even so, a part of him wasn't surprised they'd gotten this far. That would have been like being surprised that Emma's parents were still calling every hour. It was simply their nature. Just as this—this long, stubborn silence—was Dad's.

Peter remembered the first time he'd ever gotten beat up, sucker punched (not for the last time) by a bully of a kid named James McWalter as they walked home from school in third grade. Dad must have been patrolling the neighborhood in his squad car, because even as Peter staggered to his feet—a hand cupped over his eye, blinking back tears as he felt the side of his face begin to throb—Dad had the kid by the shoulders, steering him calmly over to the car, where he must have given him a good scare, because after a moment James grabbed his backpack, mumbled an apology, and darted off in the direction of his house, white-faced and trembling.

Afterward, Dad had taken Peter by the shoulder in a similar manner, half shoving him toward the squad car. His left eye was twitching, and his thumb was pressed hard against the back of Peter's neck, as if *Peter* had done something wrong. When they got home, Dad pulled a bag of peas from the freezer and jerked his chin toward the couch, all without a word.

Later, while Peter stood on his tiptoes in the bathroom, examining the pink-tinged bruise that had bloomed below his eye, Dad appeared in the doorway.

"You were holding your books with both hands."

Peter stared at him, not quite sure how to respond.

"If these kids are gonna keep bothering you, make sure to put your books in your backpack," he said. "Keep your hands ready and your eyes open. Don't be such an easy target. You have to be able to take care of yourself."

Peter nodded feebly. It wasn't until later that he realized this meant Dad must have seen him *before* he was punched, before his books went tumbling to the ground. Which meant he hadn't come to the rescue just in time. He'd seen what was happening and had chosen to wait.

123

And so when Peter finally *did* spot a flashing red light in the rearview mirror—accompanied by a whirring siren so loud it made him feel sure the whole interstate was in on it, hitchhikers and semi trucks and roadkill alike—it didn't come as much of a surprise. In fact it was almost a relief. And even as Emma began to speak fast—outlining such a litany of possible excuses and explanations that even Peter had the presence of mind to be impressed—he was still half thinking it would be easier to simply stick out his arms and wait for the officer to clap on the handcuffs, bringing this whole mismanaged expedition to a fitting end.

By the time he pulled the car onto the shoulder of the highway, he was feeling like he might very well throw up. The top was up, and suddenly the inside felt crowded and close, with Emma looking amused and the dog's tail thumping steadily against the back of his seat, making everything seem too small and impossibly stuffy. Peter sat frozen, staring straight ahead at a pink billboard for a nightclub, and so he failed to notice the policeman stepping up to the car.

"Put down the window," Emma said, looking at him with alarm when the cop knocked on the glass and Peter still didn't make a move. He was so focused on imagining what his dad might do to him once he was returned home that he didn't even flinch.

There was a second knock, this time a bit louder.

"Put. Down. The. Window." Emma's face was very close to his now, and Peter blinked at her, a bit stunned by the proximity.

"Jeez, Peter," she said, once it was clear that he wasn't in the state of mind to follow even the simplest of instructions.

She launched herself across him, straining against her seat belt, and rolled the window down herself.

"Afternoon," said the cop, a balding man whose name tag, perhaps ominously, read OFFICER HURT, and whose uniform strained against a belly that made it look like he was hiding a bowling ball under his shirt. He lowered his face so that it was level with Peter's, glancing at him and then at Emma as if puzzled by how the two of them had ended up here together.

"You were doing a fair amount of weaving back there, son," he said, turning a suspicious eye back to Peter, who hitched his glasses up farther on his nose and attempted a smile that seemed to go sorely wrong. "I'm gonna need to see your license."

As Peter fumbled through the glove compartment for his wallet, the dog took the opportunity to dart forward between the seats—eager to greet this visitor to his new home—and let out a bark so loud it rang against the sides of the car. Startled, Peter jerked away, managing to bump the back of his head hard against the cop's chin.

"What the hell?" the officer said, drawing back from the window and clapping a hand over his jaw. He narrowed his eyes at Peter. "Out of the car."

"Both of us?" Peter asked, shooting Emma a desperate look.

"Just you'll be fine."

Officer Hurt swiped the driver's license from Peter's hand before he was even fully out of the car, then stood examining it for what seemed like far too long. Peter shifted from foot to foot and tried not to look too guilty, following the flight of two crows circling overhead in the glassy sky.

A guy in an old green Chevy gave them all the finger as he drove past.

"Have you been drinking, Mr. Finnegan?" the officer asked, and even as he shook his head and croaked out a feeble "no," Peter could feel his face turn an incriminating shade of pink. The cop looked at the picture on his license and then back up at him several times, and Peter felt sure that at any minute he'd realize who he'd found, would recognize in him the same jawline and freckles and thin brown hair as his father. As the seconds wound past and neither of them spoke, it seemed impossible that he couldn't have made the connection, and it seemed that in only a moment he'd reach for his walkie-talkie to send out a nationwide bulletin, listening back as thousands of sighs of relief came in from all over the country—*That damn Finnegan kid's finally been caught in Maryland*—and the one faint whoosh of air that would be his dad shaking his head in a mixture of anger and relief.

But instead the cop looked up, twisting his mouth into a frown. "Son, I'd like to see you take nine steps along that line right there," he said. "Do you think you could do that for me?"

Peter stared at the faded white line that ran beside the metal median of the highway, then looked back at the policeman. "Um, sure."

"Wonderful," he said, nodding as if by answering, Peter had just correctly completed the first stage of the test. "And then I'd like you to turn on one foot and walk right back, okay?"

Peter opened his mouth to protest, but thought better of it and instead turned to begin the walk. His face was burning as he held his hands out unsteadily at his sides, trying not to look at Emma, who was still sitting inside the car. He squared his shoulders and set a foot down on the line just beside a ladybug, which scurried away and disappeared onto the other side of the highway. He toyed briefly with the idea of just turning himself in—rather than going through this particular kind of humiliation—but forced himself to thrust his arms out, place his heel in front of his toe, and begin to walk. At the end of the nine steps, he spun on one leg like a graceless flamingo, then made his way quickly back to the car.

"Fine," the officer said, looking unmistakably disappointed.

"I don't drink, sir."

"You're sixteen," he said, as if that meant something. "Anyway, you were driving pretty haphazardly."

"The car's old," Peter said miserably. "It can be sort of . . . tricky."

Officer Hurt looked unmoved by this. "Tricky?"

Peter watched as he began a slow circle of the car, considering it with an appraising eye and making little grunting noises here and there, his boots clicking on the pavement. Even if Peter himself weren't flagged on some kind of police network, he was sure the car must be, and his mouth went chalky as he waited for the verdict.

"And the dog?"

Peter stifled the urge to groan. *Of course,* he thought; *of course we'd dodge everything else and get caught because of a stupid stray dog.*

The back window was open a crack, and they could see the dog's black nose snuffling along its edges as he twisted his head to get a better whiff of the world outside. After a moment, he set about licking at the window, his great pink tongue covering every inch of glass as if it were a giant ice cream cone.

"It's yours?"

Peter hesitated, glancing at the car, where Emma was nodding through the window. "Yes, sir?" he said, unable to help it from emerging as a question.

The cop peered into the car once more. "He's got no collar or tags."

"No, sir," Peter agreed with a sigh.

Suddenly, Emma was out of the car too. She let the door hang open as she jogged around to the other side, her flip-flops slapping against the pavement.

"Miss, you can't just . . . ," the officer began rather futilely. "Please get back in the—"

But Emma had already sprung into action. "It's a funny story," she was saying, half laughing at the sheer comedy of it all, and Peter struggled to imitate her, attempting to arrange his mouth in a way that might suggest he was also carefree and endlessly amused.

Officer Hurt chewed on the end of his pen and waited for Emma to continue.

"Well, we've been driving a convertible, right?" she said, motioning to the blue car, where the dog was now pacing the small confines of the backseat. "And it's been hot, so we usually keep the top down. I mean, you know how it is in the summer." Peter looked on, mortified, as she patted the now dumbfounded policeman on the arm. "So we got to a stoplight yesterday morning, and he decided to jump right out of the car—the dog, not Peter," she clarified. "Anyway, we took him to the vet, just to be sure he was fine, because he had an accident as a puppy, which is why he only has three legs in the first place." Here she lowered her voice conspiratorially, leaning in toward Officer Hurt. "If you've got a three-legged dog, you need to be very careful about other injuries in case anything happens to *another* leg, you know?"

The cop just barely managed a nod.

"We had to take his collar off at the vet so that he could examine him properly," Emma continued, unfazed. "And it wasn't until we left again that we realized it, and by then we were a hundred miles away." She rocked back on her heels with a satisfied smile. "We're on our way to visit my grandparents in DC, and we don't want to be late for dinner. So we'll have to get him a new collar once we get there."

"Uh, yeah," Officer Hurt said, once Emma had finally fallen silent. "Yeah, just . . . be sure that you do. And tags, too."

"Of course, Officer," Emma said with an overly bright smile. "We really appreciate the reminder."

Peter thought this last part was a bit over the top, but Officer Hurt flushed at the show of gratitude and began backpedaling toward his car.

"Well, then," he said, bobbing his head. "Drive safely, okay?"

"Uh, my license?" Peter asked, and felt a rush of relief once the little piece of plastic was back in his own hands. They stood and watched as Officer Hurt sank back down into the driver's seat of the police car, lifted his hand in a wave, and peeled back out onto the highway.

Emma turned to Peter with a triumphant grin. "Not bad, huh?"

"I can't believe he bought that," Peter said, shaking his

head as they walked back over to the convertible.

She shrugged, sinking back down into her seat. "He wouldn't have cared about the dog, anyway. I mean, who gets busted for something like that?" she said, pushing the dog's nose away as he attempted to lick her ear. "But you were acting so fidgety and nervous about the car thing, it would've been a shame to let something as stupid as giving a ride to a stray dog be the thing to get us in trouble."

"Is that what we're doing?" Peter couldn't help asking as he pulled the car back onto the road, his hands firmly on the wheel as he navigated cautiously down the exact center of the slow lane. "Giving him a ride?"

"I don't know what we're doing with any of this, really."

Peter gave a humorless little laugh. "That's always good to hear."

"Yeah, well, things like this always work out in the end."

"Do they?" he asked doubtfully, still shaken, but Emma only grinned at him.

"Well, if not, then at least we're not stuck being bored at home. At least we're having some fun, right?"

"*This* is your idea of fun?" he asked. "Lying to the cops?"

"It wasn't lying," she said. "It was just pretending."

"There's a pretty important difference."

"Oh, come on," she said. "I'm sure the police have better things to deal with than stray dogs."

"What about stray kids?"

"You don't *really* mind," Emma told him with such certainty that Peter glanced over at her. "This is just about your dad."

"*What?*" he said, his voice coming out in a telltale squeak. He tried to laugh it off, but this too sounded strange and forced. "No, it's not."

But he knew, of course, that it was true. They were almost to Washington now, with nearly three hundred miles of highway behind them, conspicuous as the sun in the blue car and toting a lame dog who drew attention wherever they went. But nobody had stopped them, and even once someone had, there had been no sign of recognition, no dramatic arrest or abrupt ending to the trip.

And it was only now dawning on Peter that this was no coincidence. They hadn't been lucky to scrape by, and he hadn't been fooling anybody. The fact was that no one was looking for him. And he understood now that this was a choice his father had made—this decision to await his return rather than chase after him—one that Peter knew was no small sacrifice for him to make.

"I'm right, aren't I?" Emma asked, twisting to face him. "That's why you're acting all jittery? Because of your dad?"

He hesitated, about to brush away the question as he always did, hedging his bets that despite what she said, Emma wouldn't *really* be interested, or at least not for very long. But when he looked over, he saw that she was now watching him with her head tilted, an expression on her face that fell midway between affection and concern, and Peter wondered if maybe—just maybe—he'd misjudged her.

He turned back to the road ahead of them, feeling somehow lighter. They passed another police car, parked along the side of the highway, half hidden by a length of overgrown bushes so that just its headlights flashed in the late-day sun. But this time Peter drove past confidently, feeling almost invincible.

"Maybe," he said. "But I think I'm okay now."

Emma sat back and smiled. "I think so too."

chapter fifteen

It wasn't long before they reached the outskirts of Washington DC, the sprawling brownstones and colonial houses that bridged several surrounding states. Peter swung the car lazily onto an exit for the city, and Emma resisted the urge to remind him of her sister's address; he seemed so pleased at the challenge of finding it on his own, apparently reluctant to refer to the needlessly large pile of maps in the back.

The sun was low in the sky ahead, draping the trees in honey-colored light, and the roads were busy with commuters returning home after work. At a red light Peter looked at her sideways.

"Do you ever wonder what he would've been like?"

Emma yawned and rubbed her eyes. "Who?"

"Your brother."

"Oh," she said, sitting up. "I don't know. Not really."

This, of course, wasn't the least bit true; she had, ever

since she found out about him, been pondering that very question. And what she'd come up with was a wide assortment of theories and possibilities, a hypothetical resume that accounted for everything from what kinds of foods he would have hated as a baby right on up to what his grade point average might have been this year. But even to Emma this all seemed a little bit much—just a tad on the wrong side of crazy—and so she only shrugged at Peter's question.

"C'mon," he said, his voice insistent. "You must've thought about it a little bit. I mean, he was your *twin*. I wonder if you guys would have been very much alike."

"Two of *me*," she said with a grin. "Scary, huh?"

But Peter only smiled. "Not the worst thing in the world."

"I don't know," Emma said. "I mean, how many geniuses can fit into one family, right? It's nice to think he might've been more like me."

"A genius at other stuff," he said. "Like talking your way out of things."

"And wandering off."

"And avoiding people."

"And not really listening."

"Oh, yeah," Peter said, laughing now. "You're brilliant at that."

Emma smiled, sitting forward as they caught their first glimpse of DC. It wasn't anything like New York in size or scope, but there was still something about driving into a city at dusk, the lit buildings rising like silhouettes against a pale sky, a kind of glowing energy that came from leaving behind the stark emptiness of the highways. When she glanced over at Peter, she saw her own reaction mirrored in his face, and Emma realized this was all new to him, that strange and wonderful feeling when you first crest a hill and look out across a concrete landscape pulsing with shadow and light.

"Think he would've been a city mouse or a country mouse?"

"Country," Emma said. "But he wouldn't have really known it."

"Popcorn or candy at the movies?"

"Popcorn, definitely. With extra butter."

"Obviously," Peter said with a firm nod. "Dogs or cats?"

"Dogs," she said, reaching behind to give the sleeping dog a pat on the head. "Especially funny-looking ones."

"Think he would've been good at directions?"

"Better than me," she said, "but worse than you."

Peter was quiet for a moment. "Do you think . . ." He lifted one hand from the steering wheel and rubbed at the back of his neck. The red taillights from the car ahead of them reflected off his glasses. "Do you ever feel like maybe he's sort of looking out for you?" he asked, glancing over at her quickly as if to gauge her reaction. "Not in a really obvious way; I don't mean like a ghost or angel or anything like that. But just . . ."

"Just sort of out there?"

"Right," he said. "More like a feeling."

Emma nodded. "Yes."

"Yes?" he repeated, looking surprised. "Not maybe, or possibly? Just . . . yes?"

"Yeah," she said. "It's like one of your maps. There's never just one way to get somewhere, right? There are

135

a bunch of different possibilities. Some of them take you where you want to go, some bring you home, and others go somewhere else entirely. You can be really certain about really uncertain things."

"That makes no sense."

"Well, isn't that kind of the point? It would be pretty hard to believe in any of that stuff—ghosts or angels or anything else—if it all made sense."

"Yeah, well, maps are different. They're logical."

They were nearly to Annie's by now, and they made the rest of the trip in silence, Peter frowning out at the road with a look of deep concentration. Emma didn't blame him; after all, she'd insulted his entire system of beliefs. But how were you ever supposed to get anywhere if you always stuck to the same route? He spent so much time charting out the world that he barely had a chance to get lost in it.

And even now he was doing it again, proving himself better than an atlas in getting to Annie's. In spite of herself Emma couldn't help being impressed with the way he zipped around the mixed-up alphabet of streets in the heart of the city, taking shortcuts as if he did it every day.

"I guess it's a good thing that one of us is logical," she said. "You'd give one of those electronic navigational thingies a run for its money."

"GPS."

"Whatever."

"It's short for Global Positioning System."

"Don't you know how to take a compliment?" she said, though she could tell he was pleased.

They found a parking spot near Annie's house, on an

orange-tinted avenue lined with streetlamps, just beside a mostly empty pub. As Emma collected her things, she could feel the low buzz of her phone ringing inside her bag, and she knew it was her parents calling again, as they'd been doing with impressive regularity since she left Patrick's, the phone lighting up nearly every hour like clockwork, though she still hadn't worked up the nerve to pick up.

Peter stood beside the car, his arms raised skyward in a mighty stretch, and Emma held the door open to let the dog hop out, realizing for the first time that they didn't even have a leash. She crouched beside him, taking his face in both hands.

"You're gonna have to be on perfect behavior if we want to pull this thing off," she told him sternly. He wagged his tail and licked her nose.

"Should we wait to bring our stuff in later?" Peter asked, casting a nervous glance up the street. "Maybe we should try calling first? Or maybe you should go up alone?"

Emma straightened and grabbed her backpack from the trunk. "Relax," she said, starting down the block. "It's not like we're planning a robbery."

But when they found the right building—a weathered brownstone with curved windows and a hanging plant beside the door—the voice that came rasping over the intercom was about as friendly as if they *had* been planning some sort of heist.

"No solicitors."

"We're not—," Emma began, but was cut off abruptly.

"We didn't order any food, either," he said. "You're probably looking for the guy in 4A."

"No, we're looking for my sister."

There was a brief pause.

"Emma?"

"Yeah."

"Sorry," he said, the words drowned out by a loud buzz that made the door vibrate. Peter grabbed the handle. "Come on up."

"It's Charles, her boyfriend," Emma explained, breathing hard as they climbed the stairs, the dog bounding ahead of them, zigzagging along the echoing stairwell like a misguided ping-pong ball. "He's a little bit . . ." She searched for the right word, but most of them seemed to describe Peter nearly as well as Charles, and so she just trailed off, pulling herself up the banister as if it were a rope.

When they reached the fourth floor, Peter whistled for the dog, who had climbed up ahead of them. He came trotting down again, his tongue lolling out, his tail fanning the air, and took a seat beside Peter, who hung back as Emma approached the door.

"Sorry about that," Charles said, sticking his head out before she had a chance to knock. "Wasn't expecting anyone, and I'm on a deadline."

Emma waited for him to move aside or invite her in, but he was staring at the boy and the dog waiting beside her in the hallway, seemingly dismayed at the idea that they might belong to her.

"Uh, I heard you've been on the run," he said, his feet still planted squarely in the doorway. He had shocking red hair and too-pale skin and a serious look that rarely failed to disappear.

"Yeah, just call us Bonnie and Clyde," Emma said, and

Charles seemed uncertain whether or not she was humoring him. She tilted her head. "Get a lot of visitors here?"

"Some, why?"

"Because it's normally polite to ask people in."

"Right," he said, stepping aside. "Sorry."

Emma walked past him and into her sister's apartment, which looked impossibly tidier since Charles had moved in. The living room was carpeted in white, with black leather furniture and glass tables on top of which stood glass bowls filled with glass fruit.

"Is Annie home yet?" Emma asked, turning around to find that Charles had once again moved to the center of the doorway and was now blocking the entrance of both Peter and the dog, stammering and gesturing and trying to be generally polite about the whole thing.

"Hey, they're with me," she said, ducking back under his arm and trying to shoo the dog forward. Charles stuck out a foot to stop him, and the dog sniffed at it for a moment before losing interest.

"Peter Finnegan," Peter said, holding out a hand.

"Yeah, I know," Charles said, looking from the outstretched hand back to the dog. "The car thief."

Emma thumped Peter on the back. "Hey, you're famous."

"Look, I'm allergic to dogs," Charles said. "And we just had the apartment cleaned, and——" He paused to sneeze loudly, looking torn between retreating to get a tissue and standing guard at the door.

Emma folded her arms, ready to square off. She'd come this far and wasn't going to be turned away by anyone but her sister, but a moment later the heavy door behind them swung open again. The dog leaped to his feet, and Charles heaved another sneeze as Annie emerged from the stairwell, looking worn out from the day behind her and none too pleased about being greeted by the strange little entourage in her doorway.

"I wondered if you'd be showing up here at some point," she said, nodding at Charles to move his foot so she could squeeze past them all and into the apartment. She dropped her briefcase and sat down heavily in one of the leather chairs. "Mom and Dad are going nuts, you know. They seem to think you've stolen a car."

"We did," Emma said from the hallway. "Two, if you count Patrick's."

Annie sighed. "Well, you may as well come in."

Charles stepped aside, looking on wearily as the dog made sunken paw prints in the plush carpet, crisscrossing the room until he'd examined every inch of it. Peter stood awkwardly beside the couch, and Emma sat down opposite her sister.

"So," Annie said, smoothing the nonexistent wrinkles from her wrinkle-free suit, then plucking an invisible piece of lint from the couch. "Did you have a sudden urge to see the White House, or were you just really bored at home?"

"We're only passing through," Emma explained. "We were hoping maybe we could stay the night."

"Passing through to where?"

Emma shrugged, feeling this wasn't exactly the time to explain about discovering the birth certificate, not with Peter looking so out of place and Charles rubbing his red-rimmed eyes and Annie appearing less than thrilled by the situation in general.

"Are you gonna call Mom and Dad?"

Annie nodded. "I have to."

"You can't bend the rules, just this once?"

"Come on, Emma," she said, which Emma knew really meant *Grow up*. It didn't surprise her in the least that before they were formally invited in, before they were offered a drink or told to put their bags in the guest room, Annie was already up and across the room, liberating the portable phone from its white plastic cradle.

"Everyone's been going crazy," she muttered as she waited for someone to pick up. "You can't just waltz in here unannounced and then expect me to . . . Hi, Mom?"

There was silence in the too-white living room as Emma, Peter, Charles, and the dog all trained their eyes on Annie, who spun to look out the window as she listened.

"Yeah, no, she's here," she said, whirling back around as if to be sure Emma hadn't decided to make a run for it. She cupped a hand over the phone and raised her eyebrows at Peter. "You *are* Peter Finnegan, right?"

Peter nodded stiffly.

"Yup, he's here, too," she said into the phone, then held it out for Emma to take.

"You *must* be joking," she heard Mom say, as soon as she put the receiver to her ear. There was a deep grunt of agreement, and Emma realized Dad was on the line too. "Where *exactly* do you think you're going?"

"And why?" added Dad.

Mom's voice came out a few octaves higher than it normally did. "And without asking!" she yelped. "And not even a phone call to let us know you're okay! You could have *at least* had the courtesy to pick up when we've been trying you over and over and over—"

"I'm sorry; I just—"

"And taking that car!"

"That wasn't exactly me," Emma began, but was interrupted again.

"Excuse me?" Mom said. "You think Patrick's car marched itself out of New York City on its own?"

"Oh, *that* car," she said dully. "I meant the other one—"

"Don't even get me started on *that*," Mom breathed, and Dad echoed this sentiment with another hearty grumble. "I'm so sure a nice boy like Peter Finnegan would just take a car from his father's lot completely unprompted and then just happen to meet up with you somewhere. How are you getting around with two cars anyway?"

"Patrick's broke down," she explained. "I left it at the Walt Whitman rest stop on the Jersey Turnpike."

"*You did what?*" Mom said, and Emma closed her eyes to listen as she went on, outlining all the ways Emma had managed to screw up in the past few days. Her parents' reaction didn't surprise her one bit, but even as she stood there with the phone squawking in one ear, she recalled the purpose of the trip in the first place. She suddenly missed her twin brother—palpably, like a pain just beneath her rib cage, and she wondered how it was possible to miss someone you'd never even met.

Across the room Annie was watching her with a superior smile, somehow satisfied with the idea of justice being served. Charles was clutching a box of tissues to his chest as if it were a coat of armor, and Peter was looking at Emma with such apparent concern that she forced herself to turn away from her audience for fear of crying.

What had she hoped would happen, coming here? No matter what she'd told Peter, it hadn't just been about a comfortable bed and a shower. It hadn't just been a place to stay. A part of her had wanted to sit down with Annie—not the stiff, grown-up version of her sister she'd come to know, but the one she'd glimpsed during rare and unguarded moments, the one who'd giggled with her when they'd nearly knocked over the tree while putting up Christmas lights, or who'd helped with her math project over Easter. Emma realized she'd been hoping to find the sister she *wished* she had, rather than the one she actually did, and now she felt stupid and disappointed and beyond exhausted, the sheer unfairness of it all bearing down on her.

". . . and you'll drive back first thing tomorrow morning, and if you don't think you can handle that, then Dad and I will come down and pick you up ourselves."

Emma sighed. "Tomorrow morning?"

"Maybe we should give them a day to recover," Dad suggested. "Have them stay with Annie, and they can come back Wednesday morning instead."

"They need time to *recover* from gallivanting around the country?"

"You know what I mean," he said. "They've been doing a lot of driving."

"We really have," Emma chimed in, only to be met by a stony silence. "Wednesday would give us some time to rest up for the drive back."

"Fine," Mom said after a moment. "You stay with Annie

tonight and tomorrow night, and then you and Peter drive straight back home the next morning. Agreed?"

All Emma could muster was a weak, "Fine."

"And make sure Peter calls his dad and lets him know he's okay too."

Emma glanced across the room, where Peter was now looking at her with pleading eyes.

"Um, could you maybe give him a call?" she asked Mom, her eyes still on Peter, who looked so relieved it was as if he could actually hear both sides of the conversation. "Just in case Peter doesn't get through tonight?"

"He needs to call his dad, Emma. He's been worried too."

"Okay, but just in case?"

"Fine," Mom agreed. She took a deep breath, and then— as if they'd just had a heart to heart, some warm and genuine chat about their feelings—she wrapped up the whole thing by saying, "You know we love you very much."

Emma nodded. "I love you too."

And then they were gone.

When she turned back around, the dog banged his tail against the coffee table a couple of times, and Charles disappeared into the bathroom in the midst of a sneezing fit. Annie stalked off toward the bedroom, muttering something about this apartment not being a hotel.

Emma looked over at Peter and shrugged. They were clearly unwanted and in no small amount of trouble, sentenced to be shipped home again in a little more than twenty-four hours. But still, she couldn't help feeling hopeful.

"You bought us an extra day?" Peter asked with a small smile, and she nodded, grinning. A lot could happen in a day.

chapter sixteen

At breakfast the next morning Peter concentrated on his plate while Annie and Emma argued about the day ahead.

"You really don't have to come with us," Emma said. "We're fine on our own."

Peter smiled as he chewed his frozen bagel, which was still hard as a hockey puck.

"Well, it's not like you're in town that often," Annie said. "And it's not like I've taken a lot of days off."

"A lot?" Charles said, raising an eyebrow. "I can't remember the last time."

"You really don't have to," Emma said again. "We'll go wander a little, see the sights. We've been getting around just fine. Peter's like an atlas, anyway."

He smiled again, though nobody was looking at him.

Annie stood to put her plate in the sink. Even when she wasn't dressed for work, she looked somehow tailored, in nice black pants and matching heels, which clicked on the tiled floor of the kitchenette as she returned with a second cup of coffee. Peter thought she and Emma looked very much alike, though he knew Emma would be angry with him just for thinking it. But the resemblance was undeniable, and if you were to throw Emma into the shower, comb her hair back into a sleek ponytail, wrestle her into a suit, and make her take an etiquette class, you might end up with Annie: a stiffer, straighter, more precise version of her younger sister.

The two were now glaring at each other across the table while Charles picked at his grapefruit obliviously, twice managing to spray himself in the eye. Peter fed the rest of his breakfast to the dog, who was sprawled underneath the glass table, and waited for a decision to be made.

"Well, I already called in to work," Annie said. "So I guess you're stuck with me."

"You know that's not what I'm saying," Emma said. "I just don't want you to go to any trouble."

"Well, you might have thought of that before showing up without calling in the first place," said Annie. "Not to mention bringing along your boyfriend and that mutt."

"He's not my boyfriend," Emma said without even glancing at Peter, who popped a grape into his mouth, completely unbothered. Because the thing was, he *felt* like her boyfriend right now: exchanging knowing glances with Charles as the two sisters argued, bearing witness to family squabbles over breakfast. It felt a bit like playing house, and he could almost imagine they really *were* dating, that he'd been ushered home to meet her family, allowed to look in on even the most intimate moments between them, those that would otherwise remain hidden to the world at large.

And so he sat and drank his orange juice, grateful to have a seat at the table in any capacity, feeling deeply and wonderfully at home.

Emma, however, still seemed less than thrilled at the prospect of having her sister for company today, and by the time they set off toward the Lincoln Memorial, the two of them were barely speaking to each other. Every so often Annie would mutter something like "completely inconsiderate" or "just trying to be nice," and in response Emma would loop an arm through Peter's and study the surrounding buildings—grand-looking embassies and looming government offices—with a remarkable display of forced enthusiasm.

"Look at *that*," she'd say, pointing to what turned out to be a post office with the kind of awe usually reserved for monuments and other such wonders.

Peter didn't mind. He found the whole thing fairly silly—that Emma would drive all these miles to Annie's only to squander the opportunity to ask about her twin brother—but he was also secretly pleased at the way Emma was acting toward him, with a closeness that felt like a prize he'd somehow managed to win. He didn't care if it was only a reaction to Annie; he was perfectly happy to widen his eyes and ooh and aah over the rather ordinary post office building.

It wasn't long before he spotted another pay phone, a slanted structure near the river, and Annie and Emma waited patiently while he once again dialed and then hung up, but there was a strange comfort in the numbers, and words had never come easily to him anyway.

"You have a cell phone," Emma pointed out when he

walked back outside, thrusting a finger at his pocket.

"I know."

"So why do you keep using pay phones?"

"Because then he won't know it's me."

"Well, isn't that the point of calling?" she asked. "For him to know it's you?"

Peter shrugged. "It's nice to have the option to hang up."

The sun rose higher over the white city, and the three of them ambled through its maze of monuments and parks. Nobody talked much, and Peter was grateful for this. It seemed a place too important for chitchat, and he was nearly overwhelmed by it all, the buildings he'd so often seen in pictures suddenly blown up into three dimensions, towering gateways to government and democracy. They peered up at the tall spike of the Washington Monument, stared at the sun-drenched buildings on Capitol Hill, poked their heads through a fence to gaze past the landscaped lawn stretching up to the White House.

At the Lincoln Memorial, Peter stood breathlessly and ran through the words to the Gettysburg Address again— this time only in his head—and it was as if Lincoln himself had blessed the trip, like the tall man in the big stone chair was smiling down on all of them. And as they walked away from the columned building, Peter felt happy and dizzy and lightheaded all at once, closing his eyes and imagining his own map of the city, tracing a thin line across it in his mind, marking their route as others might record the day in a journal or a photo album.

They ate lunch at an outdoor café in Georgetown, squinting at each other across a table that reflected the sun like a spotlight. Once their food arrived, Peter attempted to make small talk—something he was not in the least bit adept at—but Emma still didn't seem to be making much of an effort, and the silence had become even more noticeable since they sat down.

"So," he said around a mouthful of turkey sandwich, looking from one to the other. "You guys lived here for a while when you were younger?"

Neither made any sort of move to answer, and Peter swallowed his food, thinking that he now understood why people found his own silences so frustrating.

"We moved up from North Carolina when I was a baby," Emma said finally. "Just me and Patrick and my parents, though."

"It was just after I left for college," Annie explained. "So I was already up in Boston then."

"Where?"

"Harvard."

Emma rolled her eyes, but Peter lowered his sandwich and looked at Annie with interest. "What was it like?"

"Peter's hoping to go there for a degree in Civil Warology."

"That's not a thing," he pointed out. "It would be a degree in History."

"I know," she said with a sigh. "It was a *joke*."

"It's a great school," Annie told him, ignoring her sister. "But there are lots of other great ones out there too."

"He could get in," Emma said, picking the onions off her burger, and Peter sat up a bit straighter in his seat. "He's almost worse than you guys."

Annie shot her a look. "What's *that* supposed to mean?"

"You're smart," she said. "Guess."

"What's it like there?" Peter asked, and Annie shrugged.

"It's really not all that different from the campus at home, other than being in a city."

"It *must* be," Peter said, though even as he did, he was picturing the little college on the hill, the way the afternoon shadows fell across the buildings as he passed by on the way home from school. He thought of the lake with the swans and the oak-lined paths and the sturdy little chapel that sat above it all.

And he thought of his house just down the street.

"It's not really about the campus anyway," Annie was saying now. "Wherever you go will be great, but it's more just because of what you're doing there. The place is beside the point."

"The place is never beside the point," Peter said matter-of-factly, and Annie shrugged and excused herself to go to the bathroom.

"What's up with you?" Emma asked once she'd gone.

"My dad wants me to stay home for school."

She raised her eyebrows. "Really? That's kind of sweet."

"*Sweet?*"

"Yeah, maybe he wants to keep an eye on you."

"I don't think that's it."

"He's a cop, Peter. He's probably just looking out for you."

"Yeah, because I'm so much trouble," he said, shaking his head. "Don't think so."

"Then why do you think?" Emma asked. "Because of money?"

Peter lifted his shoulders. "Maybe. I'm sure that's part of it, at least."

"But?"

"But it's not fair," he said, aware of the bitterness in his voice. "I mean, he's practically ignored me my whole life, and when he does get around to paying attention, he always ends up acting like some asshole cop. And then all of a sudden he decides I should stick around?"

"Maybe he's finally changing."

"No," Peter said, shaking his head. "He never changes."

"Well, then maybe he's *always* wanted you there. Maybe he's just never been able to say it," Emma said gently. "The thing about parents is that you always just assume they're supposed to be good at their jobs, because they're parents. But they're usually not. So this might be the only way he knows how to tell you."

Peter frowned. "Tell me what?"

"That he wants you to stay. That he'd miss you otherwise."

"But the whole point of going to college is that it's your one chance to escape where you're from. You get to start over."

"Oh, *that's* the point of college," Emma teased. "Good to know, since I thought you'd had your nose in a book all these years for fun."

"Well, it *was* for fun, actually," he said with a smile. "But you know what I mean. You're always trying to escape too."

"Yeah, but you're just talking about geography," she said. "And that's not always everything."

Later, as they walked back to the apartment, Peter noticed that Annie had picked a different route. He tried not to let this bother him, but as they headed deeper into an unfamiliar neighborhood and farther from her street, it was all he could do not to ask what was going on; it seemed impolite to question her sense of direction when she'd lived here for over ten years. So instead he studied the spidery cracks in the sidewalk, distracting himself by formulating a new map in his head.

It didn't surprise him that Emma hadn't noticed; she was too busy pretending to ignore Annie. And so when they came to a stop before a narrow house with chipped yellow paint and a faded blue door, Emma very nearly bumped into her sister.

"What's this?" she asked, frowning up at the building, which seemed to slump to one side. Through one of the downstairs windows they could see the huddled form of a sleeping cat, and the wind chimes hanging from the front porch tinkled in the breeze.

"It's where you lived when you were little," Annie said with a small smile. "It used to be white with blue shutters, and there wasn't a porch, but . . ."

Emma's face changed, her eyes widening, her mouth turning up at the corners, and she began to pace back and forth along the sidewalk, her head tipped back to take it all in. "Oh, *yeah*," she said, pointing at the driveway, the lacework of cracks in the asphalt. "This must be where I tripped when I was still learning to walk." She raked back the hair from the left side of her face to display a tiny scar that Peter had never noticed. "Three stitches. And we used to take our Christmas photo in front of that tree." She jogged over to the front corner of the house, where the cement showed beneath the wood paneling. "And that must be where Patrick crashed the car."

Peter looked on as she pinballed around the yard, and he couldn't help himself from smiling whenever she did, as if it were something contagious. It was like watching someone reclaim their past, or better yet discover it for the first time. Seeing her this way made him think, unexpectedly, of the pay phone by the river, and all the other pay phones along the way, silent and empty monuments to some great failure, whether his or his father's Peter couldn't tell.

But he wished now he'd had the courage not to hang up. All this time he'd been grateful that his dad hadn't called, but he suddenly wished just the opposite: that rather than teaching him a lesson by letting him go, letting the quiet between them stretch the length of the country, his dad would ask him to come home.

He also knew that the braver thing to do would be to stop waiting, to quit wondering, to go searching and seeking and asking. The braver thing to do was exactly what Emma was doing now. It was being determined to discover the past. It was not letting anything get in your way.

Unfortunately, Peter wasn't anything like Emma.

He watched her now, pacing the front yard as Annie pointed at the second floor of the house, which seemed to strain forward, leaning toward the telephone wires where a few birds were huddled together.

"Remember how you and Mom used to make signs welcoming me home from school?" Annie asked. "You'd hang them in the windows at Thanksgiving and Christmas. You used to be so excited to see me."

The smile slipped from Emma's face. "And you used to be so excited to come home."

Annie blinked a few times, as if unsure how to respond. "I still am," she said eventually, but something had shifted, and they stood looking at each other without knowing what to say. A bank of clouds passed overhead, pulling a shadow across the house and the little party standing outside of it, and so one by one they turned to leave, making their way back up the street single file, Annie followed by Emma followed by Peter.

"You should go easy on her," Peter whispered, feeling both brave and hypocritical at once, waiting for Emma to either snap at him or ignore him. But to his surprise she slowed down and nodded.

"It's just that she was always so close, just a city or two away, and she hardly ever visited," she said, her eyes trained on Annie's back as she led them all home. "I mean, no wonder we have nothing in common. I never got a chance to know her."

"You're family," Peter said simply.

"Maybe so, but I don't get her."

"Maybe she doesn't get you, either."

"That's the point," Emma sighed. "Nobody understands anyone else in my family, and nobody even tries. Least of all with me."

"It's not just *your* family, you know," Peter pointed out, and then stopped himself. He wanted to say more, to tell her how he suspected everyone felt a little bit alone, that maybe it was impossible to ever be fully understood, and that she wasn't the only one in the world who felt that way. But he was afraid of breaking the newfound complicity between them.

"Maybe not," Emma said. "But it sometimes feels that way."

It wasn't long before they came across a small city park where a four-man band was playing on the pavilion. Emma made them stop to listen, and as they watched, Peter could tell that the trumpet player—clearly the worst of the quartet—was struggling to keep up with the rest of them. Every so often a stray note would make itself heard amid the other instruments, and the poor man would heave a desperate breath into his horn as he limped through the song.

Peter glanced over at Emma and Annie, both looking on with a similar expression of mildest interest, their heads tilted the exact same way. Nobody else seemed to notice the lagging trumpeter as the trombonist entered the song at high volume and the saxophone kicked up at the chorus.

That was the thing about playing with a band, Peter thought. There was always someone else to rescue you when it seemed certain you might fall behind. Only the solo acts left themselves open to those kinds of disasters.

chapter seventeen

When Charles arrived home from work later, it was with a large bag of takeout food, which he and Annie set about unpacking in the kitchen.

"You guys like sushi, right?" Annie asked as an afterthought, already carrying out a large plate full of little rolls of rice with bits of raw fish peeking out the middle. The dog lifted his nose to catch a whiff, then flattened his ears and backed away with a little whine.

"Don't know," Emma said, grabbing one with two fingers. Whatever was holding it together tasted like old seaweed, and she coughed and wrinkled her nose. It was like eating a slug, the way the whole thing went slithering down her throat. "What is this?"

"It's eel," Annie said, looking amused.

"No, the part on the outside."

"Nori."

"Well, it tastes like seaweed."

"It *is* seaweed," Charles said, grabbing one for himself with a grin. "Maybe I should have ordered a pizza instead."

Annie stared at them. "You've never had sushi before?"

"I once had a goldfish named Sushi," Peter offered.

"Right," said Annie, evidently not sure how to respond to this. "So, what time are you guys planning to take off in the morning?"

Emma lowered her eyes to the bits of crab on her plate. It was hard to ignore Peter, who was looking at her with such alarm you might have thought there was a gunman standing directly behind her, and she knew he was wondering if they were really—after all they'd been through—just going to slink back home, tails between their legs, without putting up so much as a fight.

The truth was, Emma didn't know the answer to that yet.

"Whenever we get up, I guess," she said, still not looking at anyone in particular.

Annie nodded. "So what do you want to do tonight?"

"What are the options?"

"We could play a board game," Charles said, launching himself off the couch and throwing open the cabinet beneath the flat-screen TV. "Monopoly?"

"Okay, then I call the top hat," Emma announced, and Annie looked stricken.

"*I* was always the top hat," she said, and Peter and Charles exchanged a look. "Patrick was always the race car, Nate was the dog, and I was the top hat."

"How am I supposed to know that?" Emma said. "It's not like you guys ever played with me."

Jennifer E. Smith

"Maybe it's because whenever we tried," Annie said, "you always got bored as soon as you started to lose."

"Sounds about right," said Peter, and Emma shot him a look.

"Fine, then," she said. "I'll be the stupid thimble."

While they played, Emma kept a close eye on her sister, making sure she didn't snake a hand past Charles to steal money from the bank or nudge her marker forward one space too many to land on Free Parking. The Healy family had a long-established tradition of cheating in these kinds of games, applauding cleverness and ingenuity over straightforward honesty, at least within the realm of the game board.

"It's run by a pint-size millionaire wearing a tux," Dad would say whenever Emma attempted to reform them. "I'm pretty sure he expected this sort of thing."

On her next turn Annie managed to land her little top hat directly in jail. She fumbled through her piles of colored money and handed Peter—who had quite happily agreed to be banker—a fifty.

"What's this for?"

"You can bribe the banker to get out of jail."

Charles laughed. "No way."

"Don't think so," Peter said, shaking his head solemnly.

Annie looked over at Emma. "Healy family rules, right?"

Peter cleared his throat politely. "Uh, we play Milton Bradley rules."

"No way," Charles said, eyeing the top hat suspiciously. "This game's corrupt."

"That's the point," Annie and Emma said at the exact

same time, grinning at each other in an unexpected display of solidarity.

"The idea is to be clever about it," Annie explained. "But corruption rules."

"Exactly," Emma said. "Jailbirds pay off bankers to let them out early. That's just the way it is. Healy family rules."

Peter shrugged and laid the money obediently in the bank, Annie rolled the die, and the top hat went skittering further up the board as they continued to play.

Every so often Emma found herself sneaking a sideways glance at Annie, wondering if she herself looked the same way: competitive and impatient, tensed up as if ready to pounce, yet clearly enjoying herself. It had been a long time since Emma had spent time alone with her, without the rest of the family around to muddle the conversation with talk of philosophy or ethics or poetry.

She was surprised now—and a little unsettled—to see so much of herself in her sister. If you took away the clipped tone of voice and fancy vocabulary, the ramrod-straight posture and refined mannerisms, the similarities between them were undeniable. But it was something that went deeper than that too, a shared background that transcended everything else, and this somehow made Emma uneasy. All day she'd assumed they were butting heads because they were so different, but it now occurred to her that maybe that wasn't the case at all. Maybe it was because they were so similar.

Underneath the table Peter gave her foot a little kick, and Emma lurched for the die, thinking it was her turn. But when she saw that Charles was preparing to roll, she raised her eyebrows at Peter, who looked embarrassed.

"I'm still sort of hungry," he mumbled. "The sushi was good; it just wasn't . . ."

Annie stood up and stretched. "That's okay; I could use a snack, too," she said, heading toward the kitchen. "Popcorn okay with everyone?"

Peter nodded, and after a moment Emma scrambled to her feet to follow Annie out of the room. She was already tearing open a box of microwave popcorn, her head half hidden by an open cabinet.

"You can go back and hang out if you want," she said. "I'm not much of a cook, but I'm pretty sure I've got this covered."

"What about drinks?" Emma said, opening the refrigerator. "I could help with those."

Annie shrugged and pulled a few glasses from a shelf, handing them over. "Knock yourself out."

Emma filled each one with ice, and Annie leaned back against the counter as the popcorn began to heat up, little bursts of noise emerging from the microwave like distant fireworks. Out the window Emma could see the building next door, each lit square revealing a different scene: families eating dinner or watching TV, two people gesturing wildly at a toaster, a fat man with no shirt flipping an egg with a spatula. Emma's eyes skipped from one to the next, like changing television channels, and when she turned back to her own scene, it was to discover Annie watching her closely.

"So?" she asked, and Emma blinked back at her.

"What?" she said, although she already knew. Annie didn't answer, just folded her arms, and Emma took a deep breath. "I wanted to go down to North Carolina."

"To see Nate?"

She hesitated. "That was part of it, I guess."

"Well, what was the other part?" Annie asked, her mouth turned down at the corners, her green eyes searching Emma's.

"I know about Thomas," Emma said finally.

Annie stared at her for a moment, as if searching through the catalog of her mind, a lengthy glossary of schoolmates and colleagues and cousins and friends, seeking among them the Thomas who might have sent her little sister careening south in a stolen car. And when it finally registered—when it seemed to occur to her that it was *the* Thomas, the *only* Thomas, the forgotten and the unforgettable, the long-lost but never-quite-gone brother—her mouth curved into a tiny O of surprise.

"How did you . . . ?" she began, her voice low. "How long have you . . . ?"

"Not long," Emma said. "I found the birth certificate in the attic."

Annie shook her head with a kind of mechanical tempo, back and forth so steadily and for so long that Emma began to wonder whether she was okay. She didn't think she'd ever seen her sister so discomposed; Annie just stood there looking shaken and edgy and quite suddenly pale. The popcorn had long stopped popping in the microwave, but neither made a move to turn it off, and the burnt smell soon filled the kitchen. The dog padded in to investigate, the toenails of his three good paws clicking unevenly as he crossed the tile floor, and when it became clear that the smell wasn't going to be followed up with any sort of food, he curled up at Emma's feet with a sigh.

"It wasn't meant to be a secret," Annie said quietly.

"Well, you all did a pretty good job of not bringing it up for seventeen years, then," Emma said, sliding down along the cabinets until she was sitting on the floor beside the dog, who scooted over to rest his chin on her knee. To her surprise Annie joined her on the floor, sitting cross-legged in her expensive pants, the charred smell of the popcorn hovering like a cloud over their heads.

"Something's burning," Charles called out from the other room, but they both ignored him, looking evenly at each other, unsure exactly how to proceed.

A part of Emma wanted to wait until Annie apologized, until she reached for the phone to get their parents on the line so that Emma could listen as they all cried and wept and asked her forgiveness for keeping something so important from her for so many years. But the bigger part of her was tired from all the wondering, exhausted by the strain of not knowing, worn out by the guesswork and uncertainty, the near constant reminder of an unsettled past.

And so the question she finally asked was the one she'd been carrying with her the longest, since the moment she first discovered the yellowing piece of paper in the bottom of the box in the attic and saw the name so similar to hers.

"Why didn't you tell me?"

"It's not that we meant to keep it quiet," Annie said. "But after a while it just seemed easier not to talk about it, not to upset anyone. It wasn't that we were pretending it never happened. It was just a way of surviving it."

Annie was an engineer; her job was to test the weaknesses

in buildings, to guard against even the faintest of cracks. But Emma could see now how silence had worked its way through the core of her family like an invasion of termites, burrowing and gnawing until the whole thing was on the verge of crumbling. And yet Annie had stood by along with the rest of them, just watching it happen, just waiting for the inevitable collapse.

Emma shook her head. "But even now?" she asked. "So much time's gone by, and still nobody . . ."

"It just became a habit, I guess," Annie said. "I mean, every once in a while someone would try to bring it up, but everybody else would just kind of shut off. You know how our family is; it's always been easier for us to stick our noses in a book than deal with what's really going on. Dad had his poems and Mom had her research, and Patrick and Nate and I had school and jobs and futures to think about. It wasn't that we forgot. But things like that sometimes get stored away, and there never seems to be a good time to dig them up again. It hurts a lot less to keep them buried. That doesn't make it right, but it's just the way it is."

The kitchen door creaked open, and they both looked up at Charles with red-rimmed eyes. "Oh, sorry," he said, seeing them huddled on the floor. "I just thought . . . the popcorn . . . never mind." He backpedaled out of the kitchen in a hurry, leaving them alone again.

Emma looked away. She didn't know whether to be frustrated or upset by all this, whether to launch herself into her sister's arms or stay pinned against the cabinets, keeping a safe distance between them. She felt simultaneously betrayed and abandoned and grateful and sad, her heart banging hard against her rib cage.

"What happened?" she said, in a voice so small she almost didn't recognize it.

Annie looked as if she were about to cry. "We don't know," she said. "Nothing. Everything. It just happened. One night you were both fine, crying and laughing and wiggling your toes, and then the next morning, all of a sudden, he just . . . wasn't."

Emma wrapped her hand around a chunk of the dog's soft white fur as if to steady herself, swallowing hard as she watched her sister fight back tears.

Annie's voice was uncharacteristically gentle, low and gravelly and full of emotion. "You have no idea what it was like just afterward. We were all completely devastated, but Mom especially—she didn't get out of bed for weeks. And Dad walked around like a robot, talking in this awful monotone voice, like his heart had just gotten up and walked away." She paused and shook her head. "But *you* were still there, needing to be fed and changed, not knowing what happened. Patrick and I did the best we could, but I was your age at the time, you know? Nate was supposed to be spending the summer doing research in Maine, but he came home to help out. And after a while, Mom and Dad came back to us too."

Emma had been staring at her lap, absently petting the dog, but she now ventured a look up, setting her trembling mouth into a straight line.

"It was because of you," Annie said, her eyes bright. "Because you were there, needing them. Don't you see? It's never been about excluding you, or keeping you in the dark. We might be completely scattered and hopeless in the ways that count for most families, but we were there when it mattered. We needed you as much as you needed us. You brought us all back. You saved us."

When enough time had passed, Charles ventured back into the kitchen to check on them, this time with Peter in tow. Annie and Emma were still seated on the floor, only now they sat side by side, their shoulders touching, their cheeks both wet with tears.

"If this is about who gets the top hat . . . ," Charles joked, looking from one to the other, and Emma laughed a wet little laugh, coughing and wiping her eyes as they got to their feet.

Annie had a hand wrapped loosely around Emma's wrist, as if afraid to let go, and as Peter retrieved the blackened bag of popcorn from the microwave and Charles finished pouring the drinks and the dog danced around at their feet, Emma felt both lighter and heavier all at once. She felt like yelling as loud as she could until someone heard her, and she felt like her call had finally been answered. She felt like crying until there were no tears left, like running until there wasn't another step in her.

She felt scared. She felt relieved. She felt ready to go.

And later that night, once Annie and Charles had gone to sleep and the lights had been turned off and the alarms set for the morning, she tiptoed back out of the guest room and into the living room. Peter was curled beneath a blanket on the leather sofa, the dog stretched out on the floor beside him, both of them already breathing steadily.

When Emma cleared her throat, Peter jerked upright and grabbed for his glasses, which were folded on the coffee table. The dog pricked an ear in her direction but otherwise remained still, his white coat bluish in the shadows from the long windows.

"You okay?" Peter asked, making room for her on the couch. She sank down beside him and pulled her knees to her chest.

"I think so," she said. "We talked about it. About him."

Peter nodded. "I figured."

Though they'd been in the car together for days, just inches apart, she felt somehow closer to him now, his breathing soft and measured, his skin smelling of soap.

"You okay?" he asked again, but she was looking off toward the window, their blurred reflections in the glass.

"I was thinking . . . ," she said, and Peter sat up a bit straighter.

"That we'll keep going?" he asked, looking relieved. "Tomorrow morning?"

Emma smiled. "I think so, yeah. How could we turn back now?"

"We couldn't," Peter said in a solemn voice, and they both nodded, each feeling the same sense of importance, as if they'd just solidified the terms of a business deal, a verbal contract ensuring the continuation of this riskiest of ventures, the unfinished endeavor they both felt compelled to see through to the end.

chapter eighteen

They waited until Annie had left for work, until the coffee had been poured and the cereal eaten, until Charles reappeared after forgetting his wallet. They waited until the bags had been packed and the good-byes had been said and the instructions for getting home had been written down for them. And then they walked outside, got into the car, and drove off in the exact opposite direction.

Emma changed her mind three different times about whether or not to leave a note, while Peter waited patiently by the door. "It's not like she won't guess where we're headed," he offered, but in the end Emma slid the envelope onto the coffee table anyway.

Even the dog was quiet as they pulled onto the highway, sweeping beneath the signs pointing toward Richmond, Virginia. There was an unmistakable feeling that the stakes had been raised, that despite all that had come before this, it was really only now that they'd crossed some sort of line.

There are certain things in life that you'll be forgiven for, no matter how thoughtless or stupid or reckless, but if you do that same thing twice, you're on your own. And so now they both understood that there was no turning back.

This didn't bother Peter nearly as much as it seemed to be bothering Emma. The top was down on the convertible, and she had both arms resting on her door, her whole body twisted away from him so that it looked like she was contemplating an escape. It was as if they'd swapped places; Peter felt almost frighteningly happy, completely unworried about the world outside the car, while Emma looked miserably unsettled, her mouth set in a straight line, her head resting on her arms so that the wind blew her hair back like the tail of a kite.

Every so often he glanced over and tried to catch her eye, but she seemed lost in thought and determined to stay that way. And so he did his best to look concerned too—about blatantly disobeying her parents, about continuing the trip without permission, about what might meet them in North Carolina—but it proved impossible to fix his face a certain way, like trying not to laugh at church.

"Don't you sort of wish we could keep going?" he asked, when he couldn't help himself any longer. "Just drive out west, see the country . . ."

Emma swung her head around and gave him an odd look, like she hadn't quite heard him correctly, or was wishing that that were the case. She rocked back hard against the seat; behind her the dog opened one eye, then crawled over to curl up behind Peter instead.

"I can't believe I never even noticed," she said, tipping her head back to look at the open sky, an impossible shade of blue marked off only by the fading white trail from a distant plane, like the wake of a boat.

"Noticed what?" he asked, though he suspected he already knew.

"There must have been so many times when they were sad about it," she said. "It's easy to blame them for never telling me, but how could I have lived with them for nearly seventeen years and never noticed, either?"

"Sometimes it's hardest to see the people closest to us," Peter said, thinking of his dad sitting alone in his dirty tube socks with a bowl of peanuts in front of him, the tinny sounds of a baseball game drifting from a dusty television set. His throat felt suddenly tight, and whatever it was— guilt? regret? worry?—made his heart quicken.

He gripped the wheel a bit harder and tried to think of something else to say to Emma, something comforting or understanding, something impressively wise. But everything he could think of—every trite piece of advice or bit of canned wisdom—seemed to hit alarmingly close to home for him, too. After all, wasn't he just as guilty as she was? Of running away and ignoring his family? Of spending so much time wishing things were otherwise that he sometimes failed to see them as they were?

But Emma had fallen silent again, and it seemed there was little for Peter to do now other than lower his foot on the gas and ease the car into the fast lane, putting more miles between himself and his father, between here and home, between who he wished to be and who he actually was. For the moment, at least, it seemed just that easy to fall farther off the map, and for once he was more than happy to do so.

Emma's phone, which was resting in her lap, began to buzz

again, a sound now as familiar as the odd musicality of the car itself, and she stared at it for a good long while before casually raising a hand and tossing it out the side of the car.

Peter opened his mouth, glancing up to the rearview to see the tiny piece of plastic go skittering off the road. He started to pull over, but Emma put a hand on his arm.

"It's okay," she said. "Keep going."

"What'd you do that for?" he asked, incredulous, thinking what a stupid thing it had been to do, how completely and utterly Emma.

"Because," she said calmly, "they're just going to keep calling. But we made our decision. We're going."

"But what if there was an emergency?"

"Like what?" she said. "And anyway, you still have a phone."

"Yeah, but what if we got separated?"

"Why would we?"

"But just, what if?"

"We won't," she said, her tone so final that Peter decided it was easier to just drop the conversation altogether and concentrate on the road instead.

Emma's brother's house—their final destination—was tucked in the far western corner of North Carolina, where the state tapers off until it runs headfirst into Tennessee. This meant they had to cut across all of Virginia, and he frowned as he did the calculations in his head, tallying up hours and miles, accounting for his newly acquired and slightly paranoid tendency of obeying the speed limit.

"Do you want to get there today or tomorrow?" he asked Emma, who turned around and fixed him with a look bordering on disdain.

"Why would I want to get there tomorrow if I could get there today?"

Peter noticed that she'd dropped the "we" in this situation, and tried not to feel hurt. "Well, we've got about another eight hours to go," he said. "I didn't know if you'd want to get there at night." It seemed to him that there would be few things more creepy than visiting your dead brother's gravesite in the dark, but who was he to argue?

Emma gave a noncommittal grunt. "Let's see how it goes, I guess."

But even once lunchtime came and went, the silence between them remained, and so Peter kept driving. They passed several fast-food restaurants, rest stops advertising ice-cream shops, and family diners that blended in with the gray blankness of the highway. But Emma hadn't said a word in what seemed like hours, and asking whether she wanted to stop for food seemed like a fairly dangerous endeavor.

He could understand why she was upset, maybe even a little bit angry, but he wanted her to hurry up and realize that in the midst of this whole mess he was still there for her, the only one who really understood her. Even if this wasn't entirely true. Even if he was still more than a little bit mystified by her.

Even if things weren't exactly going according to plan.

Around three o'clock his stomach began to make an embarrassing amount of noise, and Peter decided it was time to step up and do something about the deteriorating state of this road trip. Plagued by worry and trailed by doubt, Emma needed to take her mind off things, to hit the pause button and forget about the grim purpose of this strange pilgrimage and have a little fun. And though Peter was well aware that he was not exactly Mr. Good Times, he was nevertheless determined to give it a shot.

According to the road signs they were thirty miles outside Roanoke, and that seemed as good a place as any. Peter cleared his throat.

"We could maybe stay around here tonight."

"It's only three."

"So?" he said. "There's tons of stuff we could do."

Emma raised her eyebrows. "Really?" she said, not bothering to hide the sarcasm in her voice. "In Roanoke, Virginia? What exactly did you have planned?"

"They have a famous transportation museum."

"I'm not even going to ask why you know that," she said. "Don't you think we've had enough fun with transportation to last us a while?"

Peter patted the wheel of the car as if to soothe its feelings. "There's also the famous star," he said. "It's eighty-eight and a half feet tall and looks like a giant Christmas decoration."

"Where do you get this stuff?"

"It uses seventeen thousand five hundred watts of power," he said, ignoring her. "It was built in 1949."

She was looking at him now with genuine astonishment.

He took this as encouragement. "It's the second largest one in the world. El Paso went and built a bigger one."

"Bastards," she said, grinning for the first time in a while.

"Yeah, well, theirs lies flat. This one is propped up, so you can see it from down below. And there's supposedly a park with a scenic overlook at the top."

"Seriously, how do you know all this stuff?"

"I just do," he said, feeling his face go hot all the way to the tips of his ears. Around the highway, beyond the pine trees that stood straight as flagpoles, clusters of mountains had begun to hitch themselves up from the land, sloping toward the sky like great whales, gray and rounded and hazy in the distance.

"You know," Peter said, "there's a campground, too."

Emma looked over at him.

"We could maybe spend the night up there."

"We don't have tents or anything."

"Well, it's not like we were planning on staying in a four-star hotel, anyway," he said. "We could just wing it."

"Don't tell me you know how to camp, too."

Peter grinned. "I've read a couple of books about it."

When they came across the right exit on the Blue Ridge Parkway, Peter swung the car off onto the spur, following the signs for the campground. They stopped at a sagging mini-mart set a few hundred yards back on a gravel drive. Two of the three gas pumps were out of order, and there was a sign out front advertising a sale on both ice and ammo. Inside, a guy about their age with too-white teeth and too-blond hair was stacking cans of soda behind the counter, and he flashed them a too-bright smile as they walked in.

"Let me know if y'all need any help with anything," he said, mostly to Emma, his eyes following her intently as she veered off toward the food aisle. Peter glared at him before hurrying to catch up with her.

"What a creep, huh?" he said as Emma thrust a bag of marshmallows at him. She scanned the rows of canned foods until she found the beans, then the packages of hot dogs and graham crackers, orange soda and dog biscuits, handing them over one by one until all of it was balanced in Peter's scrawny arms. He glanced over to see that the guy was now leaning against the counter, his eyes still focused on Emma as he chewed a piece of gum with the slow rhythm of a cow, his jaw working in methodical circles.

"He keeps watching you," Peter whispered, nearly bumping into Emma when she stopped before a rack of cheap-looking clothing. "It's weird."

She picked up a blue sweatshirt with a big red star on the front that read ROANOKE, VIRGINIA: STAR CITY. "Maybe he likes me," she joked, and Peter snorted, a feeble attempt to illustrate just how far this was from his own mind. Emma raised her eyebrows, and he felt the heat spread from his neck up into his face. He twisted the bag of marshmallows hard in his fist, feeling them lose their shape between his fingers.

She grabbed another sweatshirt from the rack and shoved it at him. "Here," she said. "One for each of us."

Peter could nearly picture the lone five-dollar bill still tucked in his wallet. "Don't you think we should save our money for something we actually need?"

"It's a present," she said, marching up to the register where the attendant was waiting, his ridiculously white teeth bared in a leering grin. "For our birthdays."

Peter dumped the pile of food onto the counter, adding a blue lighter to the pile, then slid his sweatshirt beside hers, surprised that she'd remembered. He watched the guy ring them up, half wishing—despite the sweatshirt's scratchy material and shoddy lettering—that he could put it on right away, though he at least had the good sense to be embarrassed by the significance he knew he'd attach to it because Emma had picked it out.

"This'll look nice on you," the guy said to Emma, folding the sweatshirt into a plastic bag alongside the can of beans. "Real pretty."

"It's a birthday present," she told him. "To myself."

"Happy birthday," said the guy. "A real pretty shirt for a real pretty girl."

Once they'd paid, they walked out of the store together, both struggling not to laugh until they were a safe distance away. Emma held up the sweatshirt and twirled in a circle.

"Real pretty," Peter said in an exaggerated drawl.

"Aw," she said, tossing his sweatshirt to him. "You'll look real pretty in it too."

"I think this is the first time you've ever gotten me a birthday present."

Emma smiled. "If it makes you feel any better, I forget everybody else's, too," she told him. "I'm terrible about that stuff. I must've gotten at least some of the absentminded professor genes."

"It's okay," Peter said with a grin, holding up his sweatshirt. "This top-quality half-polyester, half-cotton garment more than makes up for it."

"Only the best for you," she said as she opened the door and slipped into the car. Peter stood there a moment, not quite ready to be on the move again. The air had already lost the spongy quality from earlier in the day, shedding the mugginess of the city as they pushed farther into the mountains. There was a coolness here that pinched at his lungs and made his eyes water as he yawned and stretched and squinted out at the glancing sun and the needle-like pines.

He felt suddenly happy, and he could tell Emma was too, as if the cure to the blues were always to be found here in this run-down husk of a gas station, and they only ever had to come here to discover it.

The dog was lying on his back in the car, blinking lazily up at the sun, and he scrambled to his feet with a little grunt as they rejoined him. Just beyond the mini-mart the road took an upward swing, and the car bucked and surged as Peter coaxed it along, winding through the dense woods and up toward the campground. Emma was holding her new sweatshirt in her lap, tracing a finger along the edges of the star, and Peter's mind crept toward nightfall, nudging aside reality—against his better judgment—to consider the kinds of scenes found only in the movies: scenic overlooks and parked cars, a lanky teenager with his arm slung over some girl's shoulders, the confidence of the lean-in, the big kiss backlit by the hazy white moon.

Whenever he imagined trying to kiss Emma, the idea seemed depressingly laughable; the sheer mechanics of the thing—the subtlety of reaching over, the complicated logistics of leaning and veering and lining things up—completely impossible. Peter had never kissed a girl before, and he had great admiration for those who did it so casually. To him it seemed a feat more difficult than jumping out of an airplane or sailing around the world. Those things required nerve and daring and perhaps a little bit of stupidity. But at least they didn't involve the possibility of complete and utter rejection, or maybe even worse, a miscalculation of aim that could result in bumping heads or clinking teeth with the girl you were meant to be kissing.

He looked miserably over at Emma, who was busy sorting

through the bag of provisions for the evening. The sky ahead of them was marbled with clouds, and the wind picked up as they neared the summit, passing scattered groups of picnic tables and fire pits set along the edges of the woods. To their left the city of Roanoke stretched out in a clumsy pattern of smokestacks and buildings, and Peter remembered the giant star that glowed out across it at night and felt suddenly hopeful. Maybe the answer to all of his problems was nothing more than a darkened sky and a glittering city, a lofty perch above the world below. It seemed entirely possible that it was all just a matter of setting and location, and Peter wondered why he hadn't thought of it before. After all, he understood better than anyone the importance of geography.

chapter nineteen

In the gray pocket of time between daylight and dusk they set off from the campsite to collect wood for the fire.

"Why don't you grab some of these little twigs?" Peter told her, snapping a branch with the heel of his shoe and holding it up for her to see. He squared his shoulders and puffed out his chest a bit. "I can handle the bigger ones."

It took a lot for Emma to refrain from rolling her eyes as she watched him struggle with an enormous limb, half dragging it along the dirt path as the dog loped ahead. The woods smelled of pine needles and smoke, and they could hear other campers in the distance, the thin voices of a few girls singing, the beery sounds of men's laughter. There was a thin haze that hung just above the ground, hugging the trunks of the trees and causing the dog to reappear every so often like an unbalanced ghost.

When Peter seemed satisfied with their haul, they

carted the wood back toward the fire pit. The dog took off with one of the branches Emma dropped, and by the time they caught up, he'd reduced it to a neat pile of splinters. Peter returned to the car, which was parked just beyond a nearby picnic table, and rummaged through for some scrap paper, something to use as kindling to get the fire going. But when he couldn't find anything, he returned with one of his maps instead, and Emma scrambled to her feet, gaping at him.

"You're going to use *that*?" she asked, surprised that he'd be willing to part with it, though she hadn't once seen him refer to any of them. He had both hands poised to rip it down the center, a half smile on his face, and when Emma looked closer, she realized it was a map of North Carolina. "That's the only one we actually need!"

Peter shrugged. "I already know the way."

"But what if we get lost?" she said. "Why not tear up Madagascar or something?"

But he was already shredding it into small pieces, tucking them between the twigs set up like teepees in the charred circle of ash: first Durham, then Wilmington, then Hendersonville, the little scraps of the towns straining in the wind as if reluctant to be sacrificed.

"Once you've been somewhere, you know it," he said. "So you don't need a map anymore."

"That's great," Emma said. "Except we haven't technically been there yet. We're still a state short."

"I know," he said with a grin. "But it's symbolic."

"Well, if we end up wandering around Virginia for the next few days . . ."

Peter pulled the blue lighter out of his back pocket. "There are worse things than wandering."

"Like getting lost?"

He shrugged, his face wide open and serious. "I felt a lot more lost at home than I do here. I just never realized it. But things seem different now, you know?"

Emma watched as he got the fire started, touching the lit state of North Carolina—which was quickly collapsing in on itself—from one branch to the next, coaxing the flames to life and blowing on the kindling until the whole thing began to burn in earnest. She was never sure how to respond to this kind of honesty, though she felt much the same way. All her life she'd been hiding or walking away, doing her best to fade into the background. But things *were* different now. She could feel it the same as Peter, though she couldn't quite bring herself to say it just yet.

Peter stood back to admire his work, leaving a sooty handprint across the back of the white dog, who had ambled over to join him.

"'It is not down in any map,'" he said grandly, taking a seat on one of the flattened logs that was angled toward the fire. "'True places never are.'"

"Who said that?"

"Herman Melville," he said. "*Moby Dick*."

"My dad's favorite."

"Mine, too. After I read it for the first time, I asked my dad to throw me a whale-themed birthday party. I've never seen him so happy. He thought I'd finally gotten into fishing."

"I don't think I actually remember any of your birthday parties."

"That's because there weren't any," Peter said simply.

"I always liked planning them out, but they never ended up happening. My dad isn't great on follow-through. Not that anyone would've come, anyway."

"I might have."

Peter buried his hands in the pocket of his sweatshirt and smiled. "It's just as well. I'm not a big fan of birthday parties. It's like anything where you have high expectations." He raised his eyes to hers, giving her a long and searching look. "You're just asking to be disappointed."

Emma shifted around on the log, feeling suddenly too visible. The fire was spitting now, an orange glow pushing back the corners of darkness, and her cheeks burned from the heat. But it was more than that too. Peter was watching her with such undisguised longing, such wild hope, that it was all she could do not to bolt from the log.

It wasn't like she was blind. She knew that he liked her, had known it since the moment he pulled up to the rest stop in the blue convertible and she realized just what she'd asked of him. She thought maybe she'd even known it before he did. But until now it had seemed more of an annoyance than anything else, an added complication to the million other complications on this trip, like a bug she was forced to continually swat away.

But lately the evidence had become increasingly hard to ignore: suspicious leaning and hand-brushing, awkwardness above and beyond the usual levels of stuttering and trailing off, of blushing and blustering. Whenever boys had liked her before, Emma had either ignored them or humored them, never quite letting herself care enough to find it anything more than amusing. She'd always felt a sort of detached interest in the process, a bemused fascination with the way these things played themselves out: waiting for James Nicholson to work up the courage to put an arm around her in the movie theater, or guessing how many days it would be until Gavin Sourgen tried to hold her hand on the walk home from school. It had never been much of a problem to faze them out when they got too attached; as with everything else in her life, Emma simply took a giant step backward.

But with Peter it was different.

Emma knew she could be distant and cagey and abrupt. She knew she was wired differently from most people, that she wasn't often understood and was even less often inclined to try to understand others. But in spite of this she'd come to rely on Peter in a way she'd never allowed herself to do with anyone before. He was easy to talk to, hard to get rid of, and one of the few people who had the nerve to point out when she was being stupidly stubborn or just plain rude. Somehow he'd become the one constant in this whole uneven chapter of her life, and the idea that that could change was unsettling.

Now Peter stood up to poke at the fire with a stick. The flame made the world around it seem small; everything beyond it was dark except for the hazy glow of the giant star in the distance, which shone through the spindly trees with all the subtlety of a UFO.

"You probably would've loved the birthday parties my parents always had for me," Emma said, and when Peter glanced over at her, she could see the fire reflected in his glasses. "Their idea of a fun night is a good game of chess and an old bottle of wine, so you can imagine their version of an appropriate celebration for an eight-year-old."

"It can't be worse than the year my dad made me go kayaking and I got hit in the head with the paddle."

"Trust me, it was."

"I broke my nose," he said, raising an eyebrow, and Emma laughed.

"Well, they made *me* write a poem about what I wanted for my birthday, then had me get up and recite it at one of my dad's poetry readings in New York City. I told a roomful of literary scholars that I wanted 'stickers that sparkle, and a dog that barkles.'"

Peter laughed so hard he began to cough, shaking his head and pounding at his chest, his eyes tearing from the smoke. "I bet they saw a lot of potential in you," he said between gasps, and Emma couldn't help laughing too; for all the miserable birthdays between them, all the misunderstandings and disasters and disappointments they'd each suffered, it seemed suddenly easier not to care, now that they were together.

"If you could do anything for your birthday," she asked, once she'd caught her breath, "what would it be?"

Peter smiled at her. "This."

When he sat down again, it was on the same log as Emma, which seemed a bit closer than necessary in a circle meant for eight to ten people. She watched him lift and then drop his hand twice, as if deciding whether or not to reach for hers, and then—with a kind of slow-dawning horror—she realized he was leaning over to kiss her. His eyes were closed, and his lips were pressed together so tightly he might have been trying to avoid the dentist, but still Emma understood where this was going, and she felt such a mixture of pity and annoyance and sadness all at once that she found she'd scooted all the way to the far end of the log almost before realizing she'd planned to do it.

It took Peter a few seemingly endless moments to catch on, his eyes fluttering open in confusion. When it finally registered what had happened, he leaned back stiffly and focused his attention on his shoes. Emma swallowed hard, frozen in place on the other end of the log. She couldn't look up, because that would mean seeing the hurt on Peter's face, and so she stared at the fire until her eyes began to water, anxious for one of them to say something, to begin the conversation that would inevitably follow. But she couldn't for the life of her imagine how to begin.

The fire made the surrounding trees bend and loom like reflections in a fun-house mirror, and the dog curled up with a yawn, his bad leg pulled tight to his chest and his ears swiveling back and forth. But still they just sat there. It seemed to Emma that this was the world's longest silence, a yawning gap between them that would never end. Even the air seemed to have changed, clotted and spoiled by what had happened, and she understood that something had been tipped by her reaction. And that no matter who had been the one to lean in, no matter who had closed their eyes and reached for the other, it was still somehow her fault, and always would be.

Peter was the first to clear his throat, looking desperate to strike up a conversation, any conversation, and Emma was almost disproportionately grateful to him for being the one to do it.

"My dad would've loved this kind of thing," he said, and his voice seemed to strain with the effort. "He goes camping with his buddies all the time."

"Upstate?" Emma croaked, pleased to find that her voice still worked.

"Yeah."

"Does he ever take you?"

Peter shook his head but said nothing.

"Well, it's nice he goes out and does stuff," she said, jerking her chin toward the fire pit. "My dad has this one poem about fire, and—"

"I know it," Peter said, cutting her off. "It's one of his best."

Emma snorted. "Yeah, well. He just writes about stuff like this. He turns it into stanzas and couplets. And my mom, she analyzes things until they stop meaning anything. 'The fire represents life and the ashes represent death.' It's all just words." There was a kind of momentum to the conversation now, and Emma felt herself being swept up by it, happy to focus on something other than what had just happened. "Sometimes, I feel like they don't actually experience anything. Like they're not living so much as studying life."

"Yeah, but that's *how* you experience things," Peter said, sitting forward, his eyes now bright behind his glasses, the wounded look replaced by a kind of determination. "By digging deeper, not just accepting them for what they are. Your parents are brilliant. Look at my dad. He just sort of plods through life, drinking with his friends, going to work every morning, always the same thing. That's no way to live."

Emma stared at him. "Your dad's a policeman. He saves lives. He protects people. How can you think that's less important than the way my parents hole themselves away with their books?"

Peter stood abruptly and grabbed the bag of marsh-mallows from among their things. She could tell he was angry, though she wasn't sure if it was because of the failed kiss or the discussion at hand. He jabbed one onto a stick so hard it skidded halfway down, then considered it a moment before adding two more. It looked like a great sticky shish kebab, and he thrust the whole thing over the fire with a frown, all the while shaking his head.

"What happened to dinner?" Emma asked, watching as the marshmallows caught fire, the soft shells turning a gritty black in the flame.

Peter spun the stick in slow circles, letting it burn. "Don't you know how lucky you are?" he asked, still not looking at her, still shaking his head. "You were born lucky. You grew up lucky."

"*Lucky?*"

"Yes," he said, swiveling to face her. One of the half-melted marshmallows dripped off the stick and into the fire. "You're surrounded by some of the most interesting people I've ever met, and you're completely ungrateful for it. You have no idea how good you've got it."

"It's because I'm not *like* them," Emma said, nearly spitting the words. "What am I supposed to do? Pretend to be good at math? Pretend to care about the stupid Civil War?"

Peter slashed at the fire with his stick, the smoke twisting up into the dark. "So, what? You act all mysterious to seem more interesting?"

"What's *that* supposed to mean?"

"You're always wandering off or running away," he said. "But you're a lot more interesting when you're just being yourself, you know. When you're actually *here*."

"I have no idea what you're talking about," Emma said coldly. "Where else would I *be*?"

"You know what I mean," he said, a rough edge to his voice. "It's like you're so busy trying not to act like your family that you've never even stopped to consider that it might not be such a bad thing."

"Well, what about *you*?" she shot back, aware of the bitterness in her words. "You complain about your dad not wanting you around, and then you complain when he wants you to stay home for school. You can't have it both ways."

Peter dropped the stick, his lips parted just slightly. "Well, neither can you," he said. "You can't keep everyone at arm's length and then expect them to be there for you when you need them."

"I don't," Emma said.

"You do."

"Don't act like you know me just because you want to be like my parents," she said, suddenly furious. "And just because you'd rather hang out with them doesn't mean everyone would. Not everyone finds them so damn fascinating. Not everyone's as weird as you are."

Emma realized they were rapidly entering the territory of things that could not be taken back, and she knew she should feel guilty. But all she could muster was a small pit of anger. Because what good did it do to feel horrible about this, when she already felt horrible about so many other things? She'd never yelled at her parents, never railed against her siblings; she'd just retreated further into herself, and now it felt good to finally take it out on somebody. Suddenly, all she wanted to do was scream at the top of her lungs and pound her fists on the ground and yell because it hurt—because it had *always* hurt, and she was only just now realizing how much.

"It's not weird to be smart," Peter said, looking hurt. "Just because *you* have the attention span of a cricket—"

"I'd rather know a little bit about a lot of things than a lot about just one thing."

"But you don't," he said. "You don't care enough to bother with *anything*."

This was true, of course. Emma knew that she'd always been on the wrong side of the invisible line that separated her from her parents, from Patrick and Annie and Nate, even from Peter. But how could she tell him that the reason she always acted so disinterested in everything was because of the worry that she herself wasn't all that interesting?

"I got us all the way here, didn't I?" she said. "I've stuck with *this*, anyway."

"You wouldn't have done it on your own, though," he said quietly. "You wouldn't have done it without me."

"I'm not stupid, Peter," she said. "I can read a map too."

"That's not what I meant."

"And I could've done without the running commentary, by the way. The only reason I even called you in the first place is because I thought you were quiet."

"No, you didn't," he said, looking up at her sharply. "You called me because you had nobody else to call."

And she knew he was right.

He scowled at the fire before stooping to reorganize the careful architecture of twigs and branches, leaning away when the winds shifted and the smoke became too thick.

When he stood up again, pushing his glasses up on his nose, there was a streak of ash just below his left eye. Emma watched him pace back and forth, pulling her knees up close to her chin. And for the first time, here in the middle of the woods, she stopped thinking of this—whatever this was between them—as something she'd been nice enough to put up with, and instead began to wonder why someone like Peter Finnegan would ever want to bother with someone like *her*.

chapter twenty

Peter woke the next morning to find himself face to face with an enormous grasshopper, which directed a beady eye at him and rubbed its spindly legs together like some sort of cartoon villain. Pursing his lips Peter sucked in a breath and then exhaled, and the bug hopped away in a hurry.

It was still early, and the sun hadn't yet made its way through the thick awning of pine trees above, so the woods still looked smudged with gray in the pale dawn. He pushed himself up on one elbow, taking stock of the situation: the small pile of ashes from last night's fire, the pine needle stuck to his cheek, the sneakers he'd kicked off, which were now wet with dew. His whole left side was covered in dirt from the way he'd slept, sprawled on the hard-packed ground, and he slapped at his shirt to brush it away, without much success.

The air still smelled smoky and burnt; everything was damp and tinged with cold. Peter threw off the Roanoke sweatshirt, which he'd been using as a blanket, and got stiffly to his feet. Through the trees he could see the blue car, bright against the muted colors of the woods, its windows almost completely fogged over.

It was taking most of his energy to forget about how he'd tried to kiss Emma last night, and each time the memory rose again in his mind, it was all he could do not to go slinking off into the woods on his own, just so he'd never have to look her in the eye again. It had been mortifying and embarrassing and horrible, all the things he'd known it would be. So how, he wondered, could he have *possibly* thought it was a good idea?

The answer, he knew, was simple: He hadn't thought at all. And that was the problem with this whole trip; he'd stopped thinking the moment Emma called, had let himself be carried along like an empty-headed and lovesick idiot.

Last night's fight had ended much the same way it had started: both of them stubborn and silent and anxious to make a point of some kind. If there'd been somewhere to stomp off to, one of them undoubtedly would have, but since it was nighttime and they were in the middle of the woods—in the middle of Virginia, for that matter—there simply wasn't anywhere to go.

Up to now Peter hadn't minded when they bickered; it had usually felt more like banter than anything else, never fully serious, with a closeness about it that had been missing last night. This was different: There was no punch line, no great joke to the whole thing. They'd come too close to the truth about each other, and Peter could feel the loss of something in every single word they spoke, and even more in those they didn't.

Once the fight had given way to a tension-filled silence, Peter had grabbed the bag of hot dogs from the car, then set about roasting them with his back to Emma. When they were ready, he handed her one that was blackened and burned, but no worse off than his own. She wrinkled her nose and muttered something under her breath.

"This isn't a gourmet restaurant," he said. "You'll just have to live with it."

But she only glared at him, took two bites, then chucked the rest on the ground, looking on in silence as the dog bounded over to finish it off. Peter took a seat again—careful to pick a different log, keeping his distance this time—but even so, Emma got up with a sigh. He watched her through the darkness, feeling a mounting sense of frustration with the way she just stood there, hands on her hips, as if this decision—as well as all those before it and all those still to come—was so obviously hers to make. Everything always seemed to hinge on her word, her next move, her changes of heart and ridiculous whims. She was spoiled and bullheaded and maddeningly temperamental, so why did he always go along with everything she said?

Peter had risen to his feet with a frown, unable to help feeling like they were squaring off, eyeing each other across the weakening fire. Emma glanced behind her toward where the car was parked, and Peter decided right then to take a stand. She could have it all to herself for all he cared. He refused to be stuck in such a small space with her anyway, not when the air between them was so crowded with all that had been said. His gaze drifted across the campground, searching out a spot to sleep, formulating a plan, but before he could voice it, before he could put his foot down and make a decision and finish this night on his own terms, Emma turned on her heel and stalked off toward the car on her own, slamming the door behind her so hard that it left no question about whether or not he was welcome there anyway.

Peter stood still and watched her go, thinking that he'd never even had a chance.

Now he surveyed the same hushed woods, shivering despite the rising sun. He imagined this was what a hangover felt like: a throbbing sense of regret and a certain reluctance about making it through the day ahead.

The dog was nowhere in sight, his white coat conspicuously absent from the surrounding campsite, and so Peter set off toward the car to look for him. When he'd gone to sleep last night, the dog had been at his side, the two of them curled up beside the snuffed-out remains of the fire. And though he knew it was silly, Peter felt like he'd won at least a small battle for the night, pleased that the dog had chosen his company over Emma's.

But when he peered through the dew-covered window of the convertible, all he saw was Emma, curled in the backseat with her knees drawn close to her chest, her hair falling across her face in a way that made her look very young, and somehow very lost. Peter stood there for a long moment before turning back to the quiet forest.

For the first time he began to feel bad that they hadn't even given the dog a name—this now-constant companion of theirs—and so he picked his way through the wooded trails, calling out, "Hey, dog!" and whistling every now and again. His feet were loud against the dry branches, and he kicked at the oversized pinecones that lined the paths, his head bent and his eyes searching the gaps between the trees.

It wasn't until he began his second loop of the camp-ground that he started to worry, his stomach tightening at the idea of moving on without their new friend. He paused and took off his glasses, running a thumb absently along the foggy lenses. The trees were interrupted by thin bands of sunlight, and he held his breath and waited for the dog to emerge, wet and muddy, his tongue lolling out to one side.

"C'mon, dog," he called out again, his voice hollow and faraway. He put his glasses back on and kicked at the trunk of a pine tree, then said, "Let's go," in his best no-nonsense voice.

But there was still no sound, no echoing bark or crash-ing of branches. And despite everything—Emma and her ridiculous ideas, the muddy paw prints on the backseat of the stolen car, the policemen lining the highways with their flashing red lights, the threat of all that was behind and before them—this was the first time Peter really felt the whole thing being wrenched from his grip. It was as if he'd lost more than just a stray dog that had never really belonged to him in the first place; it was like losing the trip itself.

He walked back slowly, wishing he had a map of the park, the trees marked off as little green circles, the streams run-ning like threads across the page. He was already organiz-ing a search party in his head—breaking the mountainside into neat grids, directing imaginary rescuers to different quadrants—when he arrived back at the car. The side door was half open, and Peter could see Emma's legs, long and tanned and mosquito-bitten, hanging out the side. She poked her head out as he approached.

"Where were you?"

Peter walked around to the driver's-side door and sat down heavily in the seat beside her. "I can't find the dog."

"Did you look?"

"That's pretty much what I meant by not being able to find him."

She scowled at him. "Did you try yelling?"

"Yes."

"Whistling?"

"Yes."

"Shouting?"

"That's the same as yelling," he said. "He's not anywhere."

"Well, he's got to be *somewhere*."

"So you'd think."

Emma sighed as she got out of the car, and they both slammed their doors hard at the same time, as if it were a contest, the car rocking between them. The sky had lightened a few shades, and the birds were now singing in earnest, but although there were dozens of campers scattered in the woods around them, it somehow felt like they were all alone.

Once they'd walked for a few minutes, Peter cupped his hands around his mouth and called out for the dog again, but Emma lightly touched his arm.

"Let's listen," she said. A few squirrels ran circles around a tree branch, and the birds continued their lively chorus, but the world was otherwise still. Peter was working himself up to a sarcastic comment about Emma's usefulness in this second round of the search when they heard a low-pitched cry, followed by a familiar whine.

Emma set off at a run without even looking at him, careening straight off the path and weaving through the trees at a pace that Peter could hardly match. When he finally caught up to her, she was already bent over the dog, who was lying on his side and panting hard, his eyes wild with panic.

"What happened?" Peter said, skidding to his knees beside Emma, who was cradling the dog's one front paw in her hand. She spoke to him in a low voice, pressing his head gently to the ground to keep him from thrashing about. Peter moved over and took her place so that she had both hands free to examine the paw, and the dog whined again before resting his head near Peter's sneaker with a look of resignation.

"It doesn't look too bad," Emma said, still speaking in the same soft tone. "He cut the pad on something. See here?"

Peter craned his neck and saw that the bottom of the paw was sliced open almost entirely, a clean cut that had turned the white tufts of fur a pinkish red. Any other dog might have limped away, but without use of either of his front legs, he hadn't been able to move. Peter watched as Emma yanked off her Roanoke sweatshirt and used it to dab at the blood, all the while using her free hand to stroke the trembling dog's soft ears.

"He'll be fine, I think," she said, her mouth set in a straight line, her face as serious as he'd ever seen it. She pressed the sweatshirt against the bottom of his foot, then pulled the elastic band from her ponytail—her hair falling to her shoulders—to fasten the bulky makeshift bandage. "But we'll need to get him to a vet."

"Right," Peter said, looking down at the dog, who must have weighed at least one hundred pounds. He rose to his feet and pushed up his sleeves. "No problem."

Emma looked up from the dog and had the presence of mind to smile. "You can't carry him, you idiot," she said, jerking her head in the other direction. He hadn't noticed before that just about fifty yards away the road curved in among the trees, the pavement nearly hidden by the thick brush. "Go get the car, Hercules. And then we'll figure it out from there."

She turned her attention back to the dog, her head bent with an expression of genuine worry, of fear and urgency and alarm, but also a hint of certainty, the rarest kind of assurance. It was a look he'd never seen from her before, confident as she was, and though he knew it was important to get moving, and though he knew there was no time for this kind of thing, he stood there for a moment anyway, just watching her.

He couldn't help it.

chapter twenty-one

Emma sat with the dog in the backseat, holding his paw at an awkward angle to keep it elevated while he squirmed beside her, his eyes following hers as she spoke to him. It was hard to know what she was even saying, but the words kept coming all the same, bits of poetry she must have picked up from her dad, the words to a song her mom used to sing. She talked and she talked and she talked, and she was grateful to Peter for not interrupting her—even when he climbed back into the car after stopping at a gas station for directions to the nearest animal hospital—because there was a certain momentum to the whole thing, and she was afraid of what might happen if it broke.

The dog still made a series of pitiful cries now and then, but he had calmed down somewhat once he was lying down. Emma suspected the problem wasn't so much the cut—though that certainly wasn't good either—but the discovery that he didn't have enough good feet left to walk on.

And so she continued to rub his ears, stroke his face, run a hand along his fleecy white belly. And all the while, Peter continued to drive.

When it seemed that the dog was resting easily enough, she checked his bandage again, then looked at Peter in the rearview mirror. "Any idea if we're close?"

"Should be, yeah." He flicked his eyes up to meet hers. "You're doing great with him."

Emma nodded. "I think he's more scared than hurt."

"Still," he said. "You're keeping him calm."

They were silent after that, and Emma watched the rise and fall of the dog's rib cage, the tremble of a sigh going through him.

"I used to want to be a vet," she said after a moment, so softly that she wasn't sure Peter even heard her until he glanced up again.

"Not anymore?"

"I'm not any good at science."

"It takes a lot more than science to be a good vet," he said. "It takes passion and hard work and common sense . . ."

"It's okay, Peter," she said. "I know what I am, and I know what I'm not."

"But you don't," he insisted. "How could you? We're only sixteen."

"Almost seventeen."

He smiled. "All that stuff can be learned," he said. "What you're doing now, that's instinct. And it counts for a lot."

Emma looked down at the dog, whose eyelids were flickering, and who was making small twitchy movements with his hind legs. She ran a hand lightly over the blunt end of his missing leg, and he thumped his tail on the leather seat.

When they pulled in to the veterinary clinic, Peter ran ahead of them to get help bringing the dog inside; their efforts at carrying him earlier had been a precarious exercise in flailing and fumbling, the two of them doing everything they could not to drop him, setting him down as gently as possible every few yards. Now one of the technicians appeared with a dog-sized stretcher, and together they heaved him up and onto it.

Inside, the waiting room was nearly full. There was a droopy-eyed Lab curled up beside his owner, a man glumly clutching a large cage that housed a parakeet, and a tiny beagle puppy who threw his head back and howled at them with gusto.

"You two can wait here," said the technician, a guy who couldn't have been much older than they were. "The vet'll take a look at him and then be right out."

Emma and Peter took seats beside the man with the bird, which made a couple of piercing squawks that seemed aimed in their general direction.

"I wish we could be back there with him," Emma said, eyeing the door.

Peter leaned forward, and she could see he was reading the signs in the lobby, notices about vaccines and immunizations, puppy classes and special brands of dog food.

"How much do you think . . . ," he began, then stopped and looked at the tiled floor, his cheeks flushed. "I mean, I wasn't really thinking . . . I didn't really stop to consider . . ."

"How much this'll cost?"

He nodded.

"It can't be that bad," Emma said. "I'm sure he'll just need a few stitches. How much could it be?"

"You'd be surprised."

She lifted her shoulders. "What else were we gonna do, leave him in the woods like that?"

"No, of course not, it's just . . ."

"We'll get to Nate's house later today, so it's not like we'll need much more cash," she said. "And I've still got a bunch of my savings left anyway."

"Right."

"Do you?"

"What?"

"Have any money left?"

Peter's hand went to his pocket as if to examine his wallet, but he seemed to change his mind. "A little," he said. "But not enough for any unforeseen expenditures."

Emma realized she hadn't ever really stopped to consider Peter's finances. She knew he worked part-time at the barbershop, but she also knew he probably didn't get birthday money or an allowance like she did, and thinking back on all the meals they'd had the last few days, all the stops at gas stations and restaurants, she felt suddenly terrible for not having thought about it.

"I guess this whole trip was kind of an unforeseen expenditure, huh?" she said, and he nodded, looking somewhat embarrassed. "Look, I have enough to cover this, so don't worry about it, okay?"

"I'm as much responsible for him as you are," he said. "I don't want you to have to—"

"Peter, it's fine. Really," she told him. "And if it turns out to be *really* expensive, I've got my parents' credit card.

Which is technically only for emergencies. But I think this counts."

"I think so too," he said, his eyes wandering around the waiting room before landing on Emma. "Thank you."

The swinging door that separated the waiting room from the clinic opened with enough of a clatter to startle both the parakeet and the beagle into another song. The technician crooked a finger at Peter and Emma.

"You're up."

The vet—a middle-aged woman in scrubs—was leaning against a counter on the other side of the door, chewing on the end of a pen as she studied a clipboard.

"That's a beautiful dog you guys have," she said, looking up as they approached. "I've got him sedated at the moment, and he'll need a few stitches in that paw of his, but I wanted to first get some information from you about how it happened."

Emma nodded, eager to help.

"I guess the first order of business would be a name."

"Peter Finnegan," said Peter.

"Emma Healy."

The vet looked at them over the top of the clipboard. "I meant the dog."

"Oh," Emma said, looking helplessly at Peter. "Um, we don't . . ."

"Yeah," said Peter. "We never . . ."

"He's actually not technically ours—"

"Though he sort of acts like he is—"

"But we picked him up at a rest stop in New Jersey—"

"More like he picked *us* up—"

"But it wasn't like we stole him or anything—"

"No, he was just a stray."

The vet looked from one to the other with a little frown. "Right," she said, jotting down a note on the chart. "No name then. What I was really hoping to find out was how he got the cut. Before I get in there, it would be good to know whether it was from glass or metal, maybe a rusty fence or can, a broken bottle . . ."

"We don't actually know," Emma said, feeling like the world's worst non-owner. "He ran off this morning, and he was like that when we found him."

"So I assume you don't know anything about the original injury to the other leg?"

They shook their heads.

"Okay, then," the vet said, tucking the clipboard under her arm. "We'll go ahead and get him all fixed up. He'll have to go easy on that paw for a little while, but he should be just fine. You did a good thing, bringing him in here. Not everyone would take care of a stray like that."

"Well, he's sort of been taking care of us, too," Emma said.

The vet smiled. "Someone will let you know when we're finished back here," she said. "And in the meantime there are some brochures for different rescue groups and animal shelters in the waiting room, all of which help find good homes for strays."

Emma stared at her. "What?"

"I just assumed, since you found him, that you'd be giving him up . . ."

"No," Emma said firmly, surprising even herself. She

hadn't, until this moment, actually thought about what they'd do with the dog when they got to North Carolina. There was a strange feeling to this trip, a sense of perpetual motion that made an end point seem somehow very far away. But now that they'd come this far, now that he'd been lost and found, injured and saved, it seemed impossible to think they might leave him behind. He was as much a part of this trip as they were.

"No," she said again, shaking her head. "He's with us."

The vet nodded, looking pleasantly surprised, then walked off toward the examination rooms. And when Emma turned back to Peter, it was to find him watching her with such unmistakable pride, such open admiration, that the memory of last night's fight—the failed kiss and all that had come after it—went crashing over her again with renewed regret.

They watched the vet disappear into one of the rooms, closing the door behind her, and then they stood there together and waited for news like so many families in hospital waiting rooms: grateful for the support, relieved for the company, yet somehow feeling terribly alone just the same.

chapter twenty-two

The dog was drugged and drowsy, worn out and bandaged up, but his tail still swiped lazily at the air as they set him in the backseat of the car. The veterinary technician slid him off the gurney like he was serving a pancake, then left him dangling there, the last third of him drooping toward the balding tire of the convertible. Emma tried gently nudging him forward so that they might close the door, but the dog was too doped up to be anything more than dead weight, and it was clear that more drastic measures needed to be taken, so Peter jogged around to the other side and wiggled him into position.

Back inside they'd filled out all the necessary paperwork, and then Peter had watched as Emma paid the bill, sliding her parents' credit card across the counter while he looked the other way, trying to act casual but coming off as quite the opposite.

"Better get some tags for that dog," the vet told them as

they walked out the door, and he saw something skip across Emma's face, something like guilt, and he knew she must be thinking about the invented story she'd given the cop back in Maryland. What had been a sham of an excuse to get out of a ticket—an injured dog and a visit to a vet—had actually returned to haunt them. And wasn't that just like this trip, Peter thought. Wasn't it just so typical that all the things you never really meant to say were the very ones that came back around to you in the end?

Emma made herself a little wedge of space in the back-seat between the dog's hind legs and the door, and she sat pressed up against the side like that as he quivered in his sleep, the faintest hint of a doggy smile on his face, like a drowsy but contented drunk.

It was still early in the day, the sun sitting snugly in a bed of clouds, and Peter avoided the highways, feeling a bit like a chauffeur now that he was alone up front, responsible for the delicate cargo in back. They passed a cemetery, the kind that seems to go on forever, with neat lines of pink and gray stones like crops sprouting up from the ground. He glanced in the rearview to see that Emma was looking out too, her lips pursed and her eyes still and focused, like she was hold-ing her breath in that way children do, exhaling only once they're safely past.

When Peter thought of his mother's grave now, it was no longer a reflex or a reaction, but a conscious decision, like reciting a poem or following a recipe, something done with thought and planning. Over the years he'd trained himself in this way, corralling those parts of him that missed her, the pieces of him that still knew how to wonder. It was a luxury he didn't often allow himself, thinking of her.

But cemeteries are like mousetraps for memories, catching grief by the tail before it knows what's what. And Peter felt the yank of it now, the part of him that had been scooped out before he was even fully part of the world, so that he would always remain achingly hollow.

Once, when he was little, Peter had asked what the word "amputate" meant, and without realizing it Dad had brought a hand to his chest, thumping a closed fist softly against the dark pocket of his uniform, right near his heart.

"Cut off," he'd said, so gruffly that it had sounded to Peter an awful lot like "gutted." After that, whenever they went fishing, whenever he watched his dad slide the knife along the soft belly of a fish, Peter couldn't help thinking of the invisible damage that must have been done when his heart had been cut off, stopped short on the day Peter's mother died.

They only went to the cemetery once a year. It was just outside of town, only a couple of minutes and a few left turns in the squad car, but even so, that one awful day each July seemed like plenty to Peter. Because as much as he wished to hear stories of his mother, to crack open his father's stubborn memory, there was nothing worse than standing there on his birthday, staring down at the grave marked with the date he knew so well.

Dad would always get down on one knee and then stay there like that, still as a statue, staring at the gravestone like it had just rejected his proposal. The tree that hung over her plot dropped chestnuts like little bombshells, and the wind carried the stale scents of dried flowers and death. There never seemed to be anything for Peter to do except stand there, stiffly and awkwardly, like the only person who didn't know anyone at a party, and he wished that he hadn't arrived so late, or that she hadn't left so early, so that they might have been introduced—even if only briefly, in passing at the door—and he would then be able to greet her like an old friend.

This year Peter would be away on his birthday, still in North Carolina, or else driving back home, or perhaps somewhere else entirely. He wondered if Dad would even care. The day had always so clearly belonged to his mother, and it often seemed there was no room for anyone else.

He glanced up in the rearview mirror to see that Emma was halfway to falling asleep, her chin bobbing and then jerking upward again, her elbow slung over the dog's soft belly. He realized that neither of them had spoken since they left the animal hospital, and partly this made the car seem cozy and comfortable, and partly it just seemed inevitable, the natural petering out of whatever it was that had fueled them along the way. There was always a great dramatic flourish before a finale, the climactic upswing before the big fall. And he felt it now, the way it all seemed to be ending, like they were no longer driving so much as coasting to a halt.

It was probably stupid of him to have thought the trip would change anything. After all, leaving home behind didn't necessarily mean leaving behind the sort of person you were. And now here he was—the guy with all the maps, the one with the directions to anywhere and anything—still feeling completely and utterly lost.

It was the opposite with Emma. Peter could see that something about her had changed. Not just today—though he couldn't help being impressed by the way she'd sprung to action with the dog, so steady-handed and capable, like she'd been born to do exactly that—but this whole trip. It was like she was being put back together again, one sibling at a time, one memory at a time, and he wondered what would happen when they arrived, whether she'd finally be whole again. He envied her this, the way her story was being spun, her mysteries solved, her secrets revealed, while all of his were just waiting for him back home, nothing about them romantic or exciting or adventurous, just more of the same: a messy tangle of explanations and a very angry dad.

Peter ran his hands along the steering wheel as they crossed the state line into North Carolina. It was clear to him what his next move would have to be. He'd tried his hardest to make this work, had flattered himself into thinking that his role on this trip might be bigger than just the driver, the navigator, the polite chauffeur. If he was being honest with himself, he'd wanted to be something more. He'd wanted to be her sidekick, her partner, her friend.

And if he was being *really* honest with himself, he'd wanted even more than that.

He'd certainly tried. He'd spoken up. He'd put in his two cents and said his piece. And though he was sorry for a lot of things on this trip, trying to kiss Emma was not one of them. For once in his life, he'd failed at something. But at least he'd done it by trying, rather than standing off to the side like a coward.

Even so, he realized—several days too late—that he probably should have never answered her call in the first place, should have done this trip his own way, zigzagging from battlefield to battlefield, following the lines of history and the paths of ghosts less close to home.

And he knew now what he needed to do.

"Are we close?" Emma asked from the backseat, startling Peter, who hadn't realized she was awake. Her voice sounded very small; it was the first time either of them had spoken in hours.

"Yeah," he said. "Almost there."

"Can we go straight to the cemetery?"

Peter nodded, flicking his eyes to the left and changing lanes, heading toward the cemetery that Emma had chosen earlier in the trip, waving her finger in a little circle like a pendulum above the map. He turned in that direction now, getting off the highway onto a two-lane road that wound its way between sloping, tree-covered hills, past farmhouses and cottages and fields occupied by slow-moving horses.

The dog was awake now in the backseat, his eyes still glassy from the anesthesia, his bandaged foot tucked gingerly beneath him. Emma scratched his ears and leaned in to him, looking nervous as they got closer. At a bend in the road they came upon a small church with a raised steeple, a weather vane at the very top. Peter slowed the car, and Emma sat up to look.

It was nearly perfectly square, made of white clapboard, with a few modest stained-glass windows cut into the sides. There was a circular drive and a few overgrown bushes, and beyond that a small cemetery. Somehow, without really knowing at all, Peter was sure they'd found the right place.

The little parking lot was empty, and so Peter pulled into one of the spaces just beside the church and turned off the ignition. The dog swiveled his head in the direction of the door, as if contemplating jumping up and out, but then rolled over again with a little grunt. Emma, however, didn't move. She just sat there, her eyes as glazed as the dog's, blinking out the window. Peter couldn't tell whether he should say something or not, so he sat very still and looked out at the rows of headstones, their inscriptions worn by years of wind and rain, their edges smoothed over time.

Finally, Emma moved a hand to the door, then stayed like that, caught between moments, waiting—though for what he couldn't be sure.

"I'm sorry," she said eventually, still not looking at him. "About last night."

She didn't wait for a response, only turned the handle and stepped out of the car, and Peter watched her walk purposefully across the lawn, weaving through the headstones as if she'd always known the way. She paused before an old crab apple tree, and inside the car Peter sighed.

"Me too," he said.

chapter twenty-three

Of all the things Emma had been expecting to feel when she finally arrived at her dead brother's grave, this—this sudden urge to laugh—certainly hadn't been one of them.

After spending so many days first brooding, then stewing, she'd walked up here as if playing a part, solemn and reverent and grief-stricken, her back straight and her head held high as she crisscrossed between the scattered headstones. She'd spent days thinking about her brother, imagining what she would say when she arrived here, contemplating this recent addition to her life, who had been subtracted before she could ever come to count on him.

But now that she was here, standing before a headstone marked with a name so similar to hers—THOMAS QUINN HEALY, BORN JULY 11, DIED JULY 13—she found she had nothing to say to him. Most unexpectedly, all those things she *did* have to say, the ones she'd kept quiet about and the ones she didn't have the words for yet, all these things and more now seemed to belong instead to Peter Finnegan.

And for some reason this seemed wildly comical, like some sort of joke the world had played on her, the kind of fated, cosmic comeuppance her father might write about in one of his poems.

But when the humor of it all began to fade, Emma was left staring down at the moss-covered stone, feeling very small beneath the cottony sky. The air smelled of rain, cool and sweet, and she closed her hands one finger at a time, knuckle by knuckle, until they were tight little balls at her sides. Though she had plenty of practice at being wrong, she'd never quite become accustomed to all that came along with it, the prickle of guilt that worked its way through her like a foul-tasting medicine.

But she knew now she'd been wrong about Peter.

It was okay to find his obsession with maps a little odd, and it was fine to think he was weird because he preferred a good documentary about the Civil War to a night out at the movies. But it had been more than that. Emma felt suddenly wide awake, here among the rotting crab apples and the twisting grass. She could see now, for the first time, why she'd been so awful to him. It was one thing to count on someone who was dead and gone, to rely on an idea or a memory, a person with no real influence over her life outside of her imagination. But it was another thing entirely to have someone actually want to *be there* for you, unfailingly and unquestioningly, someone who listened carefully and told you the truth and waited patiently until you were ready to be there for them, too.

And something about that scared her.

So what she unexpectedly found herself thinking about

now—as the blossoms from the trees twirled down all around her, as the wind picked up and the birds hung suspended in the sky like misshapen kites—was Peter's mother.

Because how many hours had she spent with him in uncomplicated silence, ignoring or humoring him, thinking herself generous for enduring his company? And not once had she asked about his mom. Not once had she even thought about it.

Emma had known about her brother for less than a week, and Peter had been so quick to rush to her side when she needed him. In so many ways his loss was far greater than hers, a lifelong absence. He'd been carrying the weight of it the whole time she'd known him, and somehow Emma was only just now realizing how selfish she'd been.

She'd asked so much of him, and he'd been generous even when he didn't have to be, even when she didn't deserve it. He'd forced her to slow down and taught her to think before opening her mouth. He'd seen her impatience for uncertainty, all her bluster for lack of balance, and he'd helped her right herself again. He'd stolen a car and driven all this way; he'd pointed them in the right direction, true and unwavering as a compass, and now here they were.

All her life Emma had felt somehow incomplete, like a piece of her was missing. But standing here at the resting place of her brother—her twin, her missing piece—all she wanted to do was walk back over to the car and see Peter. Because a piece of him was missing too, and she understood now that this was why they were meant to fit. It was that simple, like the last piece of a jigsaw puzzle clicking into place, the satisfying snap of it, the long-awaited focus.

It wasn't her brother that she'd needed to make herself

whole again; it was Peter. And now that she knew, now that she finally realized it—in the same manner she came to realize most things: gradually, stubbornly, and then all at once—it was like she'd always known it, like there was never any other way it could have been.

The dog was barking from inside the car, and there was an urgency to it that made Emma feel suddenly anxious, like she'd waited too long for something that was now in danger of slipping away completely. Flustered, she knelt down beside the grave and ran her fingers along the rough stone, tracing the curved letters of her brother's name.

"Look," she said. "This isn't really a proper hello. Or good-bye. Or whatever it was supposed to be. I had a lot of things planned, and a lot I wanted to talk to you about. Our family, for one. And our birthday. And everything else. Seventeen years worth of stuff, actually."

She glanced over at the car, where Peter was leaning against the hood, his arms folded and his head cocked to take in the great map of the sky overhead, the uneven terrain of clouds and the oceans of blue in between. She turned back to the grave.

"So I guess I should be thanking you," she continued, feeling somewhat ridiculous talking to a stone. "For getting me to drive down here. It helped somehow. I think I figured out some of the stuff that needed figuring. And so I guess I just wanted to . . ." She paused, trying to figure out how to phrase this. "I guess I just wanted to meet you."

Emma sat back and blinked at the grave. The damp grass was cool against her bare knees, and she raked her hands through the dirt, wishing she'd remembered to stop and buy flowers. There was so much she'd intended to do, so much she'd planned to say; a week's worth of driving to consider it, a lifetime's worth of loneliness to prepare her.

But none of that seemed to matter anymore. She'd done what she'd come here to do. She'd said hello and good-bye; she'd met him and then let him go. And maybe it wouldn't change anything with her family, and maybe it wouldn't even change her. But Emma felt different all the same: lighter somehow, less alone. And the cause of that—Peter or her brother or her family, the many miles between here and home—didn't seem as important as the feeling itself.

She stretched to pick a dandelion, then laid it beside the stone. It wasn't a bouquet of daisies or freshly picked tulips or anything close to perfect; it was all she could do right now, but it seemed somehow appropriate all the same.

"Nice to meet you, Tommy," she said.

As she walked back toward the car, she couldn't help the corners of her mouth from turning up into a smile. There was suddenly so much she wanted to say to Peter, so many unexpected possibilities. She knew, as she hurried across the grass with a widening grin, that he'd think she was crazy; how could he not? The way she'd been bouncing from mood to mood, wanting to strangle him one minute and needing him there the next. But how could he have possibly understood her when she hadn't even understood herself? Now, suddenly, she knew what she wanted: She wanted to talk, really talk; she wanted to listen, and she wanted to change. She wanted to keep driving. She didn't ever want to stop.

But when she reached the car, bypassing her side and looping around to where Peter now sat, making notches on the worn leather steering wheel with the edge of the key, he looked up at her with an expression so grimly set and determined that she forced her mouth back into a straight line. When she opened the door, the dog lifted his head, then dropped his chin again.

Emma stared at Peter, who seemed to be summoning the courage to say something, his fingers working the key in circles, refusing to meet her eye. It occurred to her that now was her chance, that if there were things that needed to be said, then this was the moment, because the way Peter was looking at her—the vague outline of an apology forming in his eyes—made her stomach twist with the possibility that she was too late.

"Peter," she began, but he shook his head.

"Wait," he said, his green eyes focused on some point beyond the windshield, his foot tapping a nervous beat against the dusty floor mats. "Me first."

"I just —"

"Emma, please," he said, and the way he was looking at her, it was like the moment itself—so bright with expectation only seconds before—was now spiraling away, taken up by the wind like a stray leaf.

"The thing is," he began, the words coming out in a rush, "there are some battlefields around here I'd really like to see."

She knew she should cut in before he could say anything too final, before he could do anything they'd come to regret. Tell him she wasn't ready for him to go yet, let him know she was sorry, explain that she could change, that she *had* changed. But she also knew that to say those things would be to seem as bullheaded and stubborn and hasty as the person who was driving him off in the first place, and because she was determined to seem different—to *be* different—she closed her hands into little fists at her side and bit the side of her lip and waited for him to go on.

"You don't need me tagging along anymore," Peter was saying, looking as if he was still trying to convince himself of this fact. "You've got a lot of things going on with your family, and I don't want to intrude. And I figure that as long as my dad's gonna kill me anyway, I might as well see a few more things along the way. Especially since I'll probably never be allowed out of my room again."

He looked up at her as if all this was inevitable, as if he'd always known this would happen here in this shaded cemetery in western North Carolina, with the wind rearranging the grass and the trees a symphony of rasps and groans. His hair was blown sideways off his forehead, and his eyes were quiet, the bright intelligence replaced by something deeper, something sadder, maybe.

"Are you—?"

"Yeah," he said. "I'm sure."

She attempted a small smile, but she couldn't help feeling that she was falling back inside herself, despite her best efforts to stay afloat. She knew he had every right to do this, that in his position she wouldn't hesitate to do the same thing. She'd offered him so little, and even now, as she walked around to the other side of the car and slipped inside, she still couldn't bring herself to say the one thing that might fix all this, at once an apology and a wish: *Stay*.

"And hey," he said, "I could come back and pick you up afterward, unless your family . . ."

"I found my way down here," Emma said shortly. "I'm sure I can figure out a way back home."

"Okay, then," Peter said, gripping the wheel.

Emma nodded. "Okay."

He turned the key in the ignition and said it again: "Okay."

As they left, the tires bounced over the unripened crab apples that littered the drive, and the stained-glass windows of the church threw tinted colors on the hood of the car. Emma leaned an elbow on the side and told herself it was for the best, that her reasons for coming down here had had nothing to do with Peter in the first place, and that once he was gone—doing whatever it was he wanted to do, touring empty fields across the South, searching for reminders of something long since erased—she'd finally be able to focus on what was important again.

It was a short drive to Nate's house, just a few miles farther down a narrow road that cut through the kind of hills that in another season would be perfect for sledding. There were farms with hay stacked like building blocks, battered mailboxes and white fences, bird feeders and bluish grass. Emma hadn't been for a visit in years, and she'd nearly forgotten the humble charm of the little house, set near a muddy lake with a sinking dock and an overturned rowboat that looked as if it hadn't seen the water in years.

Peter turned the key and the car went silent, and Emma pressed her nose up against the window to look out at the place they'd carried her home after she was born, the place where her brother had died and her family had begun the slow process of unraveling. The horizon was crowded by the smoke-colored mountains, and from a distance the trees looked like feathers coating some giant, hunchbacked bird, the wind tipping them this way and that like needles on a scale.

The whole world smelled of pine and mulch, and they sat looking out at the house together, neither of them quite sure what to say. Emma tried not to feel so deflated, but this was what she'd come all the way down here for, and it now seemed silly and pointless. What had she hoped to do in dredging up the past? What good could that possibly have done? A part of her simply wasn't ready for the trip to be over, but another part of her knew it was more than that. She wasn't yet ready for Peter to leave.

"Well," she said.

"Well."

Peter helped gather her things from the trunk, and when they finished, she slung her backpack over her shoulder. "What about the dog?"

They both stared at the mound of white fur sprawled out across the backseat.

"I hadn't even thought of that," Peter said, rubbing at his jaw. "You should probably get to take him. I mean, you found him. And after all you did this morning . . ."

Emma shook her head. "You take him."

"Really?"

"I don't know how long I'll be staying, or how I'm getting home," she said. "You two can keep each other company."

"You sure?"

"Yeah," she said. "We can figure the rest when we get home, but I think he's gotten pretty fond of that car."

Peter thumped a fist against the hood and smiled ruefully. "Me too."

"And me," Emma said softly, and then they both stood there like that, working up to some kind of good-bye.

"So, good luck," Peter said eventually, shoving his hands

in his pockets and backing up until he ran into the car with a jolt. His cheeks reddened, and he gave a little shrug. "Let me know how things turned out when you're back home, okay?"

Emma couldn't bring herself to answer. A small and somewhat ridiculous part of her wished that he might try to kiss her again, because this time would be different. But a second chance seemed too much to hope for now, and so she managed a small nod before turning to hurry up the stone path, where she stood before the front door for a moment, trying to collect herself. Behind her she could hear the familiar rattle of the engine as Peter revved up the car, and then the bleating sound of the tires as it disappeared up the drive.

She kept her back to the street until the noise had given way to a sort of pulsing silence, until Peter was gone, and she was alone, and there was nothing more to be done except kick herself for always choosing the wrong times to be silent and the wrong times to make a fuss, for always managing to get it all so perfectly wrong.

chapter twenty-four

Though it would continue to happen often over the years, the first time Peter set off to follow Emma without an invitation was in fifth grade. Up to that point he'd spent most afternoons on his own, conducting elaborate battles across his bedroom floor, shifting a shoelace back and forth across the carpet to mark the progress of one side or the other.

But one day after school he noticed Emma heading off toward the college where her parents taught, the lofty grouping of stone buildings that had for some time been the object of intense interest for him. Hoping she might be on her way to see her parents at their offices—places he imagined as grand libraries with antique globes and row upon row of dusty, important-looking tomes—he followed, feeling quite proud of himself as he trailed along carefully behind her.

Emma wove purposefully through the throngs of college students, who all looked on with amusement at the ten-year-old girl with scabby knees and tangled hair who swung her arms with such determination. He was surprised when she walked right past the English building, then Anthropology, and then on toward the dorms, eventually going past the president's house and beyond, where the path opened up to a long field that was shaped like a comma and overgrown with weeds.

Peter hung back as she started out across it, and when he thought she was a safe distance ahead, he kicked his way through the high grass, his shoelaces undone, his backpack heavy with books, his glasses slipping down his nose. He rarely ventured up to the college, which had its own campus security force and didn't often require his dad's services. To Peter it seemed almost like a monument, untouchable and sacred and very far away from his own sagging house down the street.

At the edge of the field a wall of trees rose from the untidy lawn, and Emma disappeared into their midst, pulling back branches and picking her away along a leaf-covered path. She paused at one point, and Peter froze and held his breath, sure he'd been caught. But after a moment she kept moving, and he couldn't help following, pulled along behind her as if by some magnetic force. When she finally reached a small clearing, Peter was still a good ten yards back, but he could hear Emma—her back turned toward him—sing out, "We're here."

He stepped forward, blushing.

"Sorry," he muttered as he joined her. "I wasn't . . ."

"Yeah, you were," she said, frowning at him. "You were following me."

Not having anything to say to this, Peter poked at the

leaves with the scuffed toe of his sneaker, examining his too-short corduroys. Emma sat down beneath a tree and unpacked a thermos and an apple from her backpack.

"I only have enough for me," she said unapologetically. "I didn't know I'd be having company."

"That's okay," Peter said, sitting down cross-legged a few feet away.

The crows were circling overhead, their calls harsh and distant-sounding in the empty sky. He watched her bite into the apple, thinking how she—like him—didn't seem to have any friends at school, but though he couldn't have explained why, he knew the situation was different somehow.

"What do you do up here, anyway?"

She shrugged.

"Do you come up here every day?"

She shrugged again, and Peter stood up to circle the faded gravestones, which were covered in sap and bird droppings and stained with juice from the berries growing thickly in the surrounding bushes. There were a few dried flower petals beside one of them, but most looked largely abandoned.

"Who are these people?" he asked, stooping to read the names. "Did you know any of them?"

She shook her head.

"Then why do you come up here?"

"It's quiet," she said simply. Peter glanced over at her, thinking that her house must be fairly quiet too. He knew her older brothers and sister had all moved away, and her parents spent most of their time up at the college, or at least in their home offices, writing poems and researching speeches and lectures. He wondered what could possibly be quieter than a house that ran itself like a library, thinking of his own home, his dad half asleep on the couch with only the sound of the beer settling in its can, the soft swish as he scratched at one socked foot with the other.

"I like it here," he said, tripping along from tombstone to tombstone, studying each with interest. He could feel Emma's eyes on him with an intensity that he was unaccustomed to, and he felt a sudden tightness in his throat, like he might cough or cry without warning, like something that had been caught there for ages might now decide to come tumbling out.

He was standing before the grave of a woman who'd died in 1924 at the age of thirty, the same age his mom had been when she'd died giving birth to him, and because it was autumn and the leaves were falling all around them, because the world was a blur of red and brown and orange, because he had no one to talk to—had *never* had anyone to talk to—and because Emma was here and his dad wasn't (was never *really* there, even when he was), because of all this Peter turned to tell Emma about his mother, about the hole that had been torn in the map of his life, like a town he'd never had the chance to visit, like all the towns in the world he'd never seen and maybe never would.

But when he looked over, Emma had her head tipped back against the tree, and was humming as she watched the clouds move through the branches. Peter realized then how alone they each were. It was just that now they were alone together.

As he drove away from Nate's house, Peter gave the steering wheel a good solid pound with his fist. When the car jerked to the left with an enthusiastic little surge, he twisted to apologize to the dog, who opened one eye and yawned.

Peter couldn't believe he'd driven all this way only to end up alone again.

It was hard to believe that after all these days with Emma he hadn't picked up even a shred of her self-confidence, her reckless spontaneity and unchecked impulsiveness. He was still just as awkward and hesitant and hopeless as he'd always been, and the more he tried to overcome it, the worse it seemed to get. Just now he'd stood outside the car, and he'd waved good-bye, and he'd watched her march up to the door on her own. And then he'd driven away like a coward.

Now he considered heading south, but he'd come too far in that direction with Emma to continue on without her. East was the ocean, and Peter could already imagine a more forlorn version of himself gazing out at the open sea, angrily tossing rocks, tracing pathetic little hearts into the sand. It would all be very melodramatic, and so he thought it best to head west instead, a nod to the time-honored tradition of starting over.

There were several battlefields in the eastern part of Tennessee, strewn across the crooked edge of the state like minefields in its history. For the most part these were not like ones in the North. These were different types of memorials entirely, many of them home to crushing defeats and demoralizing losses by the South, and it seemed somehow fitting that Peter had come all the way down here to witness this.

He felt a small degree of comfort knowing he was not the first person to raise a white flag and slink away in a miserable retreat across this very land.

It wasn't long before he crossed the state line and came upon a sign for the first in a string of minor battlefields. He pulled the car off onto a gravel shoulder a few hundred yards short of the paved lot and the improvised tourist center, a small yellow trailer with an awning that flapped noisily in the wind.

It was almost evening now, and the sky was nearly colorless, a sharp wind raking the dirt along the ground. Unlike Gettysburg with its crowds of people, its maps and plaques and monuments, this was nothing more than a sprawling field, interrupted only by the occasional cluster of boulders and a couple of quivering jackrabbits lying low in the grass. There were only a few scattered cars in the parking lot, and a small group of men loitering near the visitors' center, the brims of their caps pulled low. Other than that, the world was perfectly still. Everything felt muffled and hushed and empty.

Peter left the dog asleep in the car and walked over to lean against the fence that bordered the old battlefield, the grass and the rocks and the history, the great sad nothingness of it all. He wrapped his hands around the knotted wood and rocked back on it, his head bent. He knew the story of what had happened here. He knew about the North's victory, a triumph he'd read about in stories and poems and journals. He knew that nearly three hundred men had died here, that dozens of horses had stumbled for the last time, all of it hidden by a thick cloak of fog. He knew about the muskets and the gunpowder; he knew about the cannons and the cries.

But he'd never known about it like this.

He'd never seen it from this side.

The men near the visitors' center were walking back to their trucks now, and Peter noticed that one of them had a

Confederate flag on his hat. More than one hundred years later and he still bore the scars of that loss. Peter couldn't help marveling at the way these things rippled outward, changing everyone, not just those they actually touched. Even with all the years between, all the generations later, these men still chewed on their toothpicks and gazed out at this field with damp eyes, still scraped the toes of their boots against this hallowed ground. The past still had a hold on them, no matter how thin or fragile, no matter how many ghosts had moved on or how many years had piled up since.

All his life Peter had been fascinated by history. Yet his own history remained largely unexamined. He'd never managed to find the right combination of courage and insistence to pry it away from his dad, who carried the story of Peter's mother with him as if it were his alone. And it had always seemed to Peter that there was nothing to be done about this.

But then he'd seen Emma standing in the cemetery like that—looking down at her brother's grave like she'd waited her whole life for that moment, without ever knowing it—and he suddenly wished he could say good-bye to his mother, too. Because if Emma could go to such great lengths for someone she'd never met—if she could drive hundreds of miles through so many states—then why couldn't he drive at least that far in the other direction to give his dad another chance to talk about his mom?

Emma had invented a history for her brother because he hadn't lived long enough to have a story of his own. But Peter's mother *had*, and he suddenly felt determined to know it, not just the big and important things, but the smaller ones too. Like what kind of candy she liked to eat at the movies, what her favorite animal was, whether she liked mittens and flannel sheets and secretly didn't mind the early darkness that muffled their town in the winters. He wondered whether she was good or bad with directions, whether she knew how to read a map, or if she said the numbers aloud when doing a math problem. He thought about all the years of homemade cookies and woolen socks he'd missed out on, all the good-night kisses and comforting words, and he felt an aching in his chest like a knot that refused to come undone.

The sun had fallen below the horizon now, leaving in its wake just a few strands of pink clouds, which hung low in the sky like ribbons. Peter climbed up onto the fence, his heels braced against the lower rung, and watched the shadows shift across the battlefield. He dug at a rusted nail with his thumb and kicked his heels against the fence. He tried to think of his place on a map, to pin down his exact location, to work out the coordinates, but he couldn't seem to concentrate on the precise geography of the moment, and so there was nothing for him to do but stare out across the field instead, his mind strangely quiet, unaccustomed to feeling lost.

He took off his glasses and let the world go blurry, let the shadows change shape and the bluish expanse of the field swim before him. He thought about what Emma had said back in Washington, about how certain she was that her brother was watching over her. He didn't know if he'd ever be quite as sure as that, but he found he wanted to believe it too. And he thought that maybe if he were able to fill in some of the holes in his mother's life—if he were to help his dad share those things he found hardest to voice—then somehow it might help fill out the missing pieces of their own lives too.

Peter wasn't sure how long he sat there that evening. He didn't know when the awning was folded into the trailer of the visitors' center, or when the last of the cars pulled out of the lot. At some point he heard the dog stirring in the car, and he slid down off the fence and walked back over to carry him—bent and stooped and struggling—from the roadside. And then they sat there together—Peter huddled against one of the fence posts, the dog curled at his side—watching as the sky darkened around the moon's spotlight, casting a yellowish glow across the field. Every so often Peter would wave a hand to scatter the cloud of fireflies that blinked orange in the night, but otherwise he remained still. He sat there because he had nowhere to go, and because he wasn't yet ready to go to those places he needed to be.

He slept beneath the open sky for the second night in a row, his cheek pressed against the sweet-smelling grass and the musty dirt. The stars looked silver against the navy sky, and he blinked up at them dreamily from where he was sprawled on the ground. He didn't mind the lightning bugs, didn't care for a roof tonight, and didn't hear the phone when it rang, missing all three of Emma's calls. Just before falling asleep he thought about getting his maps, but in the end he let them be.

As it turned out, being lost wasn't the worst thing in the world.

chapter twenty-five

Just after Peter drove away, after Emma squared her shoulders and took a deep breath and raised her hand to knock, the door swung open as if of its own accord, and she was left with her closed fist hanging in the air, gawking as her entire family tumbled out of the small space in a flurry of noise and activity.

"What . . . ?" she murmured, taking a step backward, looking wildly from Nate to Annie to Patrick, then behind them to where Mom stood on her tiptoes and Dad was rubbing his beard with a grin, and beyond that to Charles, who waved a tissue at her, and Megan, Nate's fiancée, who lifted a hand in greeting.

"Why are you all . . . ?" Emma attempted to ask, staring as if she'd somehow knocked on the door of the wrong house. "How are you all . . . ?"

"Just thought we'd come down for a little impromptu vacation," Mom said, breaking through her older children to give Emma a hug, then firmly steering her back through the little crowd. "See if anyone else might be inclined to show up."

"Mom . . . ," Emma began, but she wasn't sure where to even start.

Patrick clapped her hard on the back as she passed by him. "I gotta say, I'm kind of impressed you made it all the way down here," he said. "Even if you *did* leave my car in New Jersey, of all places."

"I'm *really* sorry; I just . . ."

"You couldn't have at least done better than the turnpike?" Patrick asked, though she could see he was only teasing, the corners of his mouth twisting up into a grin. "I'm sure the old girl would've preferred a beachside vacation, or a trip to Atlantic City. . . ."

"Glad you made it," Dad said, interrupting Patrick. "It sounds like quite a trip."

"I'm not really sure congratulations are in order," Mom said, throwing him a look. "But we're happy you're here."

She stepped in to give Emma another hug, but Annie beat her to it, practically throwing herself at her younger sister.

"Happy early birthday," she whispered, and Emma realized she'd nearly forgotten that it was tomorrow. What had only a week ago seemed reason enough to flee from home was now a quiet and unassuming milestone, an ending to a journey rather than the start of something new.

The house was cool and dark, and Emma felt suddenly tired, like she'd walked all the way from New York, like she'd sailed half the globe, like she was the last weary survivor of the world's longest journey. They moved inside together, a knot of people clogging the narrow entryway with laughter and hugs, with shakes of the head and wagging fingers.

Emma attempted to find a beginning to her story, an explanation for the events of the past days, but it proved nearly impossible with an audience like this one, her whole family buzzing all around her. They were all talking over one another in an attempt to explain each of their unlikely presences here—an impulsive, last-minute road trip from New Jersey for Patrick, a worried drive from DC for Annie and Charles, an anxious flight for Mom and Dad—and Emma sat down on the couch in the living room and stared out the window at the spindly trees and the stippled lake and tried to assemble her own story, answers she didn't yet have to questions she didn't yet feel ready to think about.

There was so much they wanted to know.

"Where's Peter?"

"What happened to that dog?"

"Did you forget how to use the phone?"

"How could you not tell us you were leaving?"

"Hasn't anyone ever explained to you the finer points of car theft?"

Emma tried to respond as best she could, grateful that their happiness at seeing her and their relief over her safety seemed, at least for the moment, to have forestalled the inevitable lecture about her little road trip, the doling out of a punishment and the consequences that were sure to follow. But even so, she couldn't help breathing out again when they began to disappear one at a time: Mom to call Peter's dad and let him know his son was still at large, Nate to fire up the grill, and the rest of them to get started on dinner.

Emma sat there and listened to the sounds coming from the kitchen, overwhelmed and still a bit stunned to see all of them here at once. She could hear someone cutting vegetables and pulling down pots, the singing of the gas stove, and the screen door banging shut. A cork popped, two glasses clinked, and then a short burst of laughter rang out. It had been so long since her family had all been together: Last Christmas, Nate and Megan had been delayed by a snowstorm, and by the time they arrived at home, Annie and Charles had already left to go back to DC for work. It was always this way; they were always just barely missing each other. But now here they were, all gathered together; each of them had dropped their classes and studies, their jobs and responsibilities, and they'd done it all for *her*.

Emma knew she was still in trouble, that there were still discussions and consequences to come. But right now it was as if that had all been forgotten. As if the past days had never even happened. She was suddenly surrounded by all the many people who cared about her, in the place where everything had started, which was all she'd really ever wanted in the first place.

So then how was it possible, she wondered—her thoughts drifting to Peter—that in the midst of so many people she could still feel so terribly lonely?

Later, Emma offered to help set the table, escaping into the quiet of the dining room. She could hear the rest of her family joking around in the kitchen: Patrick pelting sponges at Annie, Nate rattling off statistics about energy efficiency in dishwashers, and Mom helping Megan wash vegetables as she explained the basis for her latest research project.

Charles had set out after Dad, who'd wandered off to the backyard garden when nobody was looking.

Emma circled the table, taking her time with the silverware, grateful for a quieter task and wondering if maybe she wasn't cut out for this kind of togetherness. Perhaps her tendency to be alone wasn't so much because nobody was ever around—as she'd always thought—but rather because she preferred it that way. Maybe she had a natural propensity for silence. Maybe she was doomed to a life of solitude.

"Well, at least your table manners didn't fall by the wayside when you decided to become an outlaw," Nate said, and Emma looked up to see him leaning against the doorframe between the kitchen and the dining room. He was the tallest of all of them, skinny and serious, altogether too intelligent for Emma. Patrick was exasperating and Annie intimidating, but Nate had always seemed unapproachable in a way the others hadn't, like a respected professor who is equal parts admired and feared.

"You could've called, you know," he said, pulling out a chair and watching her circle the table as she laid out the silverware. "I would've bought you a plane ticket."

"That wasn't the point."

"No," he said, looking at her thoughtfully. "I suppose it wasn't."

Emma could still feel him watching her as she folded napkins, and it was as if he was weighing something, making up his mind about her.

"Do me a favor, will you?" he asked finally, and she glanced up at him with raised eyebrows. "Can you run down to the basement and grab the silver salad bowl? It's on one of the far shelves."

"We already have one," Mom said, walking in to set down a basket of bread.

Nate shook his head. "I think we need another."

Mom frowned. "Why?"

"Just go grab it for me, will you?" Nate asked Emma, and she shrugged, heading off around the corner and down the stairs.

The basement was dimly lit, with only a few cobwebby bulbs dangling from between the rafters. It took a minute for Emma's eyes to adjust, and she blinked around at the musty room, the shelves of drooping cardboard boxes labeled with the names of each of her siblings. This house had been the family's before it had been Nate's, and though the upstairs was now quite distinctly his, the basement still held years of unsorted junk, a staggering collection of memories both priceless and worthless.

Emma walked in a slow circle around the room, running a hand along the dusty shelves, her eyes watering. There was a box of dolls with no clothes, old board games with missing pieces, a shoebox full of marbles and pebbles and sea glass. She stood on her tiptoes to unearth an empty fish tank that had grown moldy with years, two deflated soccer balls, and a tiny baseball mitt.

In the back corner she spotted the salad bowl. It was old and tarnished and not something she particularly wanted to eat out of, but she picked it up anyway, measuring the weight of it in her hands. Just before she turned around, she noticed the box underneath it, which had *T and E* written in faded marker across the side.

Emma wiggled it out from the cupboard, blowing the layer of dust from its lid and setting it on the old corduroy couch that had probably been down here at least as long as she'd been alive. And then—for the second time in just about a week—she held her breath as she opened the box.

Last time, when she'd found the birth certificate, she hadn't been expecting anything. But now she understood what *T and E* meant, was aware of the sorrowful implications behind a box so thick with dust; she guessed nobody had been able to bear looking at whatever was inside for a very long time. And sure enough, what she found made her hands tremble too. Nestled inside were two small baby blankets—one pink, the other blue—and two teddy bears, both still soft and new. There were two delicate rattles that looked as if they'd hardly been used, and a pair of matching knit caps, everything in twos, everything a set, as if her family hadn't been able to bear using one without the other. Emma picked each item up, one at a time, trying to imagine what it must have taken to pack these things away, to have bought them with so much hope, only to abandon them again so soon. It nearly broke her own heart seeing the tiny monogrammed letters across the edge of each blanket.

Beneath these was a small silver-edged photo album, and Emma breathed in at the sight of the engraved names: Tommy and Emma. She found herself almost smiling; she'd known somehow that he would have been a Tommy. And if he'd never had the chance to become any of the other things she'd imagined for him, she was happy that at least he'd had that.

The pictures inside had been taken mostly in the hospital: Mom smiling wearily from the bed, a baby crooked in each arm; Dad kneeling beside her with a goofy grin; Annie as a teenager, kissing baby Emma on the forehead; Patrick,

237

lanky and buck-toothed at fifteen, holding up Tommy's hand in a miniature high five. In the back of the album were a few pictures taken on the front lawn of this very house, of Mom and Dad each holding one of the twins up to the camera, bundled so that just their noses were visible. There was something different about her parents here; their eyes hadn't yet misted over in the look Emma had always thought of as a kind of distant dreaminess, but which she now recognized for what it was: the scar left behind by their loss.

She wasn't sure how much time had passed when she heard footsteps on the sagging wooden stairs, and she thought about leaping into action, shoving the box back in its place and lunging for the salad bowl, pretending none of this had ever happened, but instead she stayed where she was—beside the open box, holding a photo of the entire family: Mom, Dad, Nate, Annie, Patrick, Emma, and Tommy—and waited until Mom appeared, pausing on the bottom step with a look on her face that was impossible to read.

Emma wasn't sure what to expect. Her family wasn't accustomed to delving into anything too far outside the realm of academia, and now that she'd uncovered the one subject that had been kept the most quiet of all, now that the lid was—quite literally—off the box, Emma wasn't entirely sure how to proceed.

But if what she'd expected was another lecture, another point-by-point explanation dictated by logic and reason, then she'd been wrong. Instead, without saying a word, Mom crossed the basement and sat down beside Emma on the couch, leaning over to plant a kiss on her forehead. She didn't say she'd been wrong, and she didn't tell Emma why it had been kept a secret. She didn't apologize, and she didn't explain. Instead she took the photo album gently from Emma's hands and opened it up to the first page. And then she began to talk.

"This was just a few hours after you were both born," she said, her voice soft and thick. "I was in labor for twelve hours. You two were worse than any of the others."

Emma watched her mom's face as she flipped the pages, the lines that gathered at the corners of her eyes like a map of their shared past.

"You came out first," she said, tracing the edges of the picture with her thumb. "And then he . . ." She cleared her throat, then started again. "And then Thomas—Tommy— was next. His face was all pinched like he was already annoyed at being last." She smiled and blinked hard. "He would've been a real handful. He was already stubborn as anything. It's amazing how much you can tell, even in such a short time."

Emma leaned in closer to look at the pictures, so close that their elbows were touching, and after a few minutes she rested her cheek on her mother's shoulder, looking on as Mom colored in the pictures, filling in the missing pieces.

When she paused, Emma sat up to look at her.

"I study anthropology," Mom said, her eyes focused across the room. "I lecture about grief, about burial rights and the way people mourn." She turned to face Emma. "There's no right way to do it. Some people need to talk, and others just can't. Some need to remember, and others to forget. It's different for everyone."

Emma nodded, and Mom shook her head and smiled.

"And some need to steal a couple of cars and drive a few hundred miles."

"Some do, I guess," Emma said ruefully.

There was another soft thud from the top of the stairs, and they both looked over to see Dad's loafers, and then a moment later his balding head, as he ducked to see who was below. And by the time he reached the bottom step—his face already changing as he realized what they were looking at—Patrick was pounding his way down as well, muttering all the while about how hungry he was before falling silent when he saw the scene on the couch. One by one they were joined by the rest of the family, until all of them were huddled together in the damp coolness of the basement. Nate nodded at Emma from where he sat on the arm of the couch, and she smiled at him gratefully. Upstairs the burgers were burning on the grill, and the salad was growing limp in its bowl. But no one seemed in a rush to leave as Mom began to speak again.

There were no asides about poetry or statistics, no interruptions or jokes. They were too busy listening and remembering, digging through the old collection of memories, the lost history that belonged to each and every one of them. It almost felt as if the story couldn't have been told until now anyway, until they were all gathered here together like this.

And just like that, Emma knew what she wanted for her birthday.

chapter twenty-six

When Peter woke the following morning, it was to discover two state troopers leaning against the blue convertible and regarding him suspiciously. Their patrol car was parked just behind it, the squawking of the radio interrupting the otherwise quiet morning. Beside him the dog lifted his head and then—seeing nothing of any great interest—rolled back over in the soft grass with a contented sigh.

Peter ruffled the back of his hair and yawned, stumbling to his feet. His clothes were wet with dew, and when he glanced out over the battlefield, he found it hidden by a low-hanging fog.

"Morning," Peter said with a nod, ambling past the officers. He fumbled for his keys, then opened the passenger-side door and reached in to grab his cell phone, which was making a series of faint beeps, its battery nearly dead. He rested an elbow on the roof of the car, scrolling through his missed calls, his heart picking up speed when he guessed it was Emma who had been trying to reach him.

One of the troopers cleared his throat a bit too forcefully, and Peter glanced up at them over the top of the car. He raised his eyebrows and tried his best to look polite, though all he felt was impatience. There suddenly seemed about a million places he should be, a thousand things he needed to say and do, and two people he wanted desperately to talk to. He didn't have time to exchange pleasantries with two cops in pointy hats and overly tight pants.

"Everything okay?" the taller one asked from behind aviator glasses that made him look like a bug. Peter slipped his still-beeping phone into his pocket and nodded.

"Are you lost, son?" the other asked, and Peter couldn't help laughing at this, shaking his head and grinning like an idiot, because for once in his life he *was* lost, yet somehow, as unlikely as it seemed, he'd never felt quite so sure of himself.

"I'm okay," he told them, feeling a lot like Emma, bold and spontaneous and unafraid. "Just passing through."

"Where to?"

Peter shrugged, still smiling. "I don't know yet."

"Right," said one of the troopers, reaching for his walkie-talkie. He glanced at his partner, rolling his eyes in Peter's direction with a remarkable lack of subtlety. "Your call, Joe."

Joe was now working a sesame seed out of his front tooth with his pinky, having apparently lost interest. He shrugged. "Don't let it happen again, kid. This is a historical site, not a hotel. If you can't tell the difference, I suggest you get yourself a map next time."

Peter nodded, just barely managing to keep a straight face. "Thank you, sir," he said, appropriately solemn. "I'll do that."

The messages had been left only minutes apart, all of them late the night before. In the first she didn't even bother with a greeting, instead launching right into a recitation of the names of important battlefields—in alphabetical order—until the phone cut her off. In the second one all she said was, "Those are all the places I promise to go with you on the way home if you'll just do me one last favor." Then there was the sound of yelling in the background, and a whistle, and then muffled laughter before the message came to an abrupt end.

Peter had pulled over to the side of the road once he was far enough away from the state troopers, and he now jabbed at the numbers on the keypad, impatient for the next message.

"Sorry about that," it began, and Peter smiled almost reflexively when he heard her voice again. "I think my brothers have somehow reverted to whatever age they were when we last lived in this house. Anyway, this is my version of an apology. I know it's not great, but I've messed up everything else so far, so why not this, too?"

There was a short silence, and then she cleared her throat. "So, look. I'll go to all those old battlefields with you, and I'll even listen to you talk about them, if you'll come back here and pick me up first. There's just one more thing I need to do before heading home. I understand if you're already too far away, or if you just don't want to come, but it would mean a lot if you did. So if you can, meet me back

243

in the cemetery tomorrow morning at eleven, okay?"

Peter kept the phone pressed to his ear long after it had gone dead. And then, once he felt prepared to start the engine again, he swung into a U-turn and pointed the car east once more.

But there was one thing he needed to do first, and it wasn't long before he found himself standing outside a gas station that straddled an intersection between two backcountry roads, a small cabin of a building that was now more yellow than white. There was a phone booth to one side of it, looking out of place between an air pump and a display of feeble-looking purple flowers, and Peter heaved open the rusted door.

The glass was clouded with dirt, and the space inside smelled of cigarettes and stale beer. He dug in his pockets for change while reading the various inscriptions etched into the booth, proclamations of love and hate and revenge and loss, all tagged with initials in an effort to leave some kind of mark on the world.

Nearly out of money by now, he only managed to come up with two nickels and a penny, and so he picked up the phone and dialed the operator to make a collect call. He played with the cord as he listened to it ring, wondering what his dad had been doing, wondering if he'd even accept the call. But a moment later his voice came over the line, a gruff hello that gave nothing away.

"Hi, Dad," Peter said, making an effort to keep his voice steady. "How are you?"

There was a brief pause. "How *am* I?"

"Yeah, sure. How are you?"

"What is this, a social call?" Dad practically spit into the phone. "How *am* I? Well, I'm *fantastic*. Really. Just wonderful."

"That's great," Peter said, bobbing his head.

Dad snorted. "And where the hell are *you*? Or is it too much to ask to be kept up to speed on your whereabouts?"

"I'm in Tennessee. On my way back to North Carolina."

"On your way back to North Carolina," Dad muttered. "I guess there's no point in asking why you're not on your way back to New York?"

"I'll get the car back to you, Dad," Peter said. "I promise."

"It's not the car I'm worried about," he said, and then coughed into the phone and made a few grumbling noises.

They seemed to run out of things to say then, caught between polite conversation and their usual dynamic, between anger and relief.

"So what the hell are you doing down there, anyway?" Dad asked eventually. "Looking at colleges or something?"

Peter pressed the phone harder against his ear. "Not really, no. I've got some time to decide all that."

"I heard there are some good ones down there."

"I know," he said. "But I've been thinking it probably makes sense to apply to a whole bunch of different places. Just to see what happens."

"What about . . . ?"

"Yeah," Peter said, nodding into the phone. "There, too."

"But I thought you hated this place," Dad said with barely disguised shock. "I thought you'd rather be anywhere but home."

"Maybe that was just because I'd never been anywhere else," he said. "It's hard to know what you're looking for when you've only seen one thing."

"And now what? You're some big-time traveler, ready to come home?"

"Guess so," Peter said, tracing a heart that had been carved into the glass door of the phone booth. He thought carefully about his next words. "People can change, you know, Dad," he said hopefully, but when, after a few beats of silence, it didn't appear that there would be a response to this, he sighed and leaned against the booth. "Anyway, I wanted you to know I'm not coming home just yet. I've got to go back and get Emma first."

To Peter's surprise Dad seemed to find this funny, the phone rattling with his laughter, a sharp and unfamiliar sound. "Is *that* what this is about?"

"What?"

"A girl?"

Peter hesitated. "Would that make it better?"

"Trust me, son. Nothing's gonna make this better," Dad said, but Peter could hear the amusement in his voice all the same, an overtone of relief that seemed to stretch across the conversation. It wasn't coming easily, and it wasn't yet natural for them. But it was there all the same.

"You know," Dad said after a moment, "I once drove your mother up to the Canadian border. Only trip we ever really took. We didn't tell our parents either, and by the time we got back, we were in a whole world of trouble."

Peter found he was holding his breath. "Why?"

"Why do you think?"

"No, I mean why did you go?"

"She wanted to see Niagara Falls." He fell quiet, and Peter let the silence swell between them. "She had a thing for waterfalls. Kind of the way you are with those damn battlefields, I guess."

Peter smiled. "You'll have to tell me about it sometime."

There was a long pause, and for a moment Peter was afraid his dad wasn't going to answer. But then his voice came over the line again, his words soft and measured.

"Yeah," he said. "I guess I will."

It seemed impossible that it had only been twenty-four hours since he and Emma last stood in this same cemetery before this same sleepy church. The sky was clear this morning, cloudless and breezy, and the place now had an almost springtime feel to it. A group of sparrows scattered when Peter pulled the car into the drive, taking a few hops before launching themselves skyward, and the sun made everything looked tinged in gold, as if lit up from the inside out.

There were several more cars in the lot today, so Peter had to park farther from the cemetery. He was so concentrated on scanning the churchyard, so distracted in searching to see if Emma was there yet, that it wasn't until he got out of the car that he realized he'd parked next to a familiar light-blue convertible very much like the one he was driving.

He stood there staring at it, the keys dangling from his hand, before collecting himself enough to take a look at the license plates, which were—as he suspected—from New York. Behind him the dog let out a few sharp barks, hitching himself up from the seat, wobbly on his bandaged leg. Peter opened the back door and half lifted him from the car, the dog wriggling with excitement as he hobbled jerkily around the parking lot until he found a suitable patch of grass, where he promptly flipped onto his back and rolled around until his fur was streaked with mud. Peter was still watching him with amusement when Emma came barreling around the side of the church.

When she saw him, she stopped short, skidding a few inches on the pavement.

"You came," she said, her eyes widening.

Peter grinned. "Happy birthday."

It seemed to take a moment for it to register that he was actually there, but once it did, Emma's face broke into a smile too, and she came bounding over to greet him. When she threw her arms around his neck, the two of them breathed matching sighs of relief, both thrilled to be reunited and surprised to find the other equally as happy. There no longer seemed any point in pretending otherwise.

And before he could overthink or overanalyze it— before he could begin to worry or calculate or consider all the things that could possibly go wrong—Peter closed his eyes and leaned in and kissed her. And much to his surprise—without bumping heads or getting tripped up by any of the other thousand or so catastrophes that might have occurred—he found that she kissed him right back. Her hair smelled of pine needles, subtle and sweet, and for the first time in his life Peter understood what the opposite of lost was: that it had nothing to do with maps or directions or staying on course; that it was, in fact, nothing more than being found.

But sooner than he would have liked, Emma took a step backward. "I'm sorry," she said without looking at him, and Peter felt his stomach drop.

"I guess I'm the one who should be apologizing then," he muttered, shaking his head and trying not to feel disappointed. "*I* kissed *you*."

"No," she said with a frown. "Not about *that*. That was okay."

Peter grinned. "It was?"

She nodded impatiently. "I meant that I'm sorry about everything else. You came on this trip without asking any questions, and you were so great about everything, and I should've been a better friend to you."

"It's fine—"

"No," she said. "It's not. You've been so good to me. Not just this past week, but always. Nobody's ever really taken the time to . . ."

"What?"

"I don't know," she said. "Get to know me, I guess."

"I know you," he said with a smile. "I've always known you."

Emma blinked a few times, and Peter could see that her eyes were damp. He raised a hand to brush away a stray tear with his thumb—thinking this would be both incredibly considerate and exceedingly romantic—but somehow managed to step on her toe in the process, tripping forward and poking her in the eye instead.

Emma gave a little yelp, clapping a hand over the left side of her face, and Peter stared at her in horror. "I'm so sorry," he said in a rush. "I was only trying to—"

"It's okay," she said, and he was relieved to see she was

half laughing at him, sniffling a bit as she took her hand away from her face and blinked a few times.

"I guess I shouldn't have pressed my luck."

Emma shook her head. "It's fine, really."

The dog ambled over, stepping gingerly on his bad paw, and Emma kneeled down and took his face in her hands as he shoved his nose into her neck, slobbering and drooling and wiggling all over.

"He's feeling better today."

"I'm glad," Emma said, beaming at the dog. "And I'm glad you both came."

She stood up and walked over to the blue convertible, popping open the trunk and rummaging through until she found a box of candles. "You guys are the last to arrive, actually. My whole family showed up yesterday, every single one of them. And since they were all down here already, I thought this would be a nice place to celebrate my birthday."

"It is," Peter said. "I'm glad you invited me."

"Yeah, well, I know what a sucker you are for birthday parties," she teased, handing him the candles and slipping the keys back in her pocket.

He laughed as he reached over to close the trunk for her. "I guess I can make an exception for this one."

"Good," she said. "Because everyone's waiting for us."

He flipped the box of candles around in his palm, then held it up. "So," he said. "Think your brother would've liked birthday cake?"

She hesitated, but just for a moment, before reaching for his hand. "I do," she said, looking at him intently. "And what about your mom?"

"I don't know about that," Peter told her, closing his

fingers around hers as they began to walk. "But I do know she liked waterfalls."

"Waterfalls?"

He nodded.

"That's almost as weird as battlefields."

"It is," he said with a grin. "It's exactly as weird as battlefields."

When they rounded the corner, Peter could see that there was a small table set up near her brother's grave, right there among the tall grass and the fallen crab apples. There were flowers and gifts and balloons, and there was a cake in the center of it all, around which Emma's entire family stood, waiting for her. The dog skipped out ahead of them, loping along with a funny little gait, his tail streaming behind him and his ears pricked forward. He reached the group first and took a seat in their midst, waiting as Emma and Peter approached—hand in hand as they crossed the lawn, tired and happy as any two survivors of a great expedition—and then he lifted his head and let out a deep, echoing bark to welcome them home.

Acknowledgments

Many thanks to all those who helped me find my way here: Jennifer Joel, Emily Meehan, Binky Urban, Rob Wooldridge, Kelly Smith, Courtney Bongiolatti, Niki Castle, Kristyn Keene, Andy Barzvi, Jenni Hamill, and my parents, Jim and Kathy Smith.